Defeated. Balding. Pung ..... ~~~ is troubled and cuts a pitiable figure in his job on a long-distance train.

His road to salvation starts in a most unlikely place: his bathtub.

Ride the rails with Mister Bob in *Rub-A-Dub-Dub*, through an underworld of private squalor, public shame and sublime bodily landscapes.

Robert Wringham is a humour writer so devoted to his craft that he almost won the Leacock Medal but failed. He is the editor of *New Escapologist* magazine and the author of seven books including *A Loose Egg*, *Melt It!*, and *Stern Plastic Owl*. Novelist Luke Rhinehart described him as "the best prose writer I know" while comedian Stewart Lee has called his books "mini masterpieces." *Rub-A-Dub-Dub* is his first novel.

Also by Robert Wringham

Humour Collections
A Loose Egg
Stern Plastic Owl

Fringe History
You Are Nothing
Melt It! The Book of the Iceman

"Escapology"
Escape Everything!
The Good Life for Wage Slaves

Rub-A-Dub-Dub

Rub-A-Dub-Dub

A Picaresque

Robert Wringham

This edition first published 2023

P&H Books Ltd.
Glasgow, Scotland

www.poniesandhorsesbooks.com

Cover art by Thomas MacGregor
Cover and text design by Rob Westwood

A CIP record for this book is available from the British Library

ISBN 978-1-910631-78-2

Printed in Great Britain by Mixam

ATTENTION SCHOOLS AND BUSINESSES:
P&H books are available at quantity discounts with bulk purchase
for educational, business, sale and promotional purposes. For
information, please email P&H on info@poniesandhorsesbooks.com

The words "pink mooning bum" appear in this novel. They are dedicated affectionately to my sister, Katy.

The rest is for George Cockcroft.

Far from hot baths he was indeed, poor man. And not he alone. Nearly all the *Iliad* takes place far from hot baths. Nearly all of human life, then and now, takes place far from hot baths.
—Simone Weil

Man is born free but is everywhere in trains.
—Tiresias

A chill wind riffled through what remained of his hair. He sank down under the water to keep warm, but temptation got the better of him and soon he was peeking over the side again, his breath steaming into the night. He marvelled at the city lights twinkling beneath the belly of the clawfoot: the floodlit spires of St Giles' loomed large while the castle stood darkly upon its rock. He wowed at the grand ruins on the hill and derisively tossed sudsy foam into the grounds of the palace. Down in the streets were the rumbling pubs he knew well and, beyond them, the bricky expanse of the New Town giving way to Leith and to the Firth of Forth. Above him, a golden moon gazed down benignly while constellations unknowable winked in and out.

"This is the 6Music News at seven o'clock with me, Katherine Cracknell," said a voice from everywhere. He shrugged the dream off roughly. He would never remember it.

"Prince Andrew is facing a barrage of criticism," said Katherine Cracknell, "over a so-called plane crash interview in which he tried to set the record straight about his relationship with convicted sex offender Jeffrey Epstein..."

Oh, shut up, he thought.

"...who took his own life in a New York jail earlier this year..."

Shut up, he thought again, his hand crashing down onto the "stop" button. *Shut up, shut up, shut up.*

His sweaty Y-fronts on the floor resembled a deflated hot air balloon. He picked them up and put them back on. It was time to go to work.

October

One

"Hoy, Mister Bob!"

The neighbourly call, an assassin's bullet, echoed down and around the corkscrew of the stairwell.

This Mister Bob was a 53-year-old bachelor. He was balding slightly and his moustache was stupid-looking but he hadn't the courage to shave it off in case he looked even worse without it, like a pink mooning bum. Also, he had an odour problem. It had been on his list of problems to solve for so long—decades, probably—that he barely noticed it anymore, though most other people did. The slightest hint of exertion sent his sweat glands into party time, a tendency exacerbated by the terrible clothes he was made to wear for work. It was a shame for Mister Bob and it was also a shame for anyone who shared a lift with him.

The tenement building in which Mister Bob lived did not have a lift, which is why we find him this afternoon sweltering his way down the stairs.

"Good, ah, afternoon, um, Pavel," Mister Bob called up to Pavel's landing. He tried, unsuccessfully, to affect a jovial, friendly attitude and a not-at-all-clapped-out demeanour.

A further problem of Mister Bob's was that he struggled to complete a sentence without an "ah" or an "um" or some other disruptive interjection. It wasn't his fault. He was nervous.

It wasn't his fault that he was balding or that he smelled bad either. Nor, for that matter, was it his fault that he was alone. He just hadn't lived a very lucky life so far. The shower above the bathtub in his rented flat didn't work properly because the boiler that was supposed to heat the water was old and cheap. It was always something like this: small problems on top of small problems, the culmination of which had cemented his pitiful, smelly bachelor status. It all felt eternally beyond his control. He sometimes wondered where this tumbling snowball of trouble had first begun to roll, that if perhaps he could isolate the mistake that had eventually led him to be so balding and smelly, he could begin to undo it all by working backwards. But he never got very far in this analysis before some other stupid thing came out of the accumulation of his problems that required urgent attention. It sometimes felt to Mister Bob that his life wasn't really his own. But if it wasn't his, whose was it?

"Bring me back a little something, yes, Mister Bob?" called Pavel over the central handrail, his oniony words falling all over Mister Bob's head and down the back of his neck, "a little something from the *Magnificent Caledonian Sleeper*, yes?"

Pavel liked trains. The way he said "Magnificent Caledonian Sleeper" sounded better than an advertising slogan, utterly in love and without a trace of irony.

Mister Bob did not like trains.

The reason Mister Bob did not like trains was that he worked on them all day long and, often, all night long as well. Ever since he'd grudgingly accepted the job, he'd found it lonely and undignified. He knew there was something deeply unnatural about being in such constant motion. Plus he was pestered by passengers all the time and the exertions of cleaning up their mess and answering their questions while pretending to be their friend made him sweat like an unrefrigerated leftover beetroot.

Unlike the Pavels of the world, Mister Bob had not given trains much thought before finding himself employed by a railway company, and now he had to think about trains for money almost every day and then he had to think about trains without remuneration whenever Pavel caught him in the hallway. And Pavel always caught him in the hallway. To Pavel, Mister Bob was practically a celebrity. He, to Pavel, was one of the blessed ones who could spend hours and hours zooming up and down the length of the country on a splendid, gliding, cheerfully tooting "locomotive".

"Yes, ah, Pavel, um, of course, ah, if I, um, remember."

Mister Bob, thought Mister Bob, *for crying out loud.*

Mister Bob did not think with "um" or "ah." It was only when the words came to his lips that he felt compelled to string them together with "um" and "ah." Mister Bob's mind was fast but his body and his mouth were slow.

Nobody else called him "Mister Bob." They called him, simply, "Bob" or "Robert" or sometimes "Mister Forrester" before they lost respect for him. He was uncertain as to why Pavel should call him "Mister Bob." It was most likely a misplaced gesture of deference due to his connection to trains. Or perhaps, Mister Bob theorised wildly, that Pavel came from a country where the conventions of surnames and forenames were reversed. He wasn't sure where Pavel came from. Russia, he thought. Or maybe Belarus. Or Estonia or Ukraine. Mister Bob didn't think any of those countries had reverse surname conventions. It was President Putin, wasn't it? Not Mister Vladimir. But now, since Pavel has introduced us to Mister Bob, "Mister Bob" is how we will know him. Poor Mister Bob. Wrong place, wrong time. As usual.

Mister Bob was on his way to work. Tonight, he was scheduled to work the sleeper service between Inverness and London Euston. It was scheduled to leave Inverness at 21:00 and to travel through the night. Unfortunately for Mister Bob, he lived in Edinburgh.

And he didn't live in the middle of Edinburgh either. He lived in Portobello, a pretty seaside suburb some fifteen minutes in a car or half an hour by bus or an hour of breathless trudging from Edinburgh's main Waverley Station. As such, Mister Bob's commute to work today looked like this: he'd take the 124 bus from Portobello Town Hall to Waverley Station, then he'd take the 17:49 from Waverley to Dunblane, and then he'd take the 18:49 from Dunblane to Inverness.

Mister Bob's neighbour, Pavel, could have told you all about Mister Bob's commute, parroted in a trance-like state, after hours upon hours of studying railway company timetables just for fun. He might have struggled to remember which bus number you'd need to begin with though because Pavel's love was reserved for trains, not buses.

All in all, the commute took four hours and nine minutes, during which time Mister Bob would read a book brought from home and, when his brain could no longer absorb the words of the dead, he would stare vacantly out of the window while twitching his moustache. He was not paid for this time in transit, but nor was he expected to pay for his tickets. The railway company presumably saw this as fair.

Mister Bob would begin his shift officially at Inverness and, finally on the clock as a "team member," the lowliest pay grade in the entire railway company, he would wipe seat-back trays with a damp cloth and collect half-drained coffee cups and blu-tack "out of service" notices onto toilet doors all the way down the hunched spine of Britain, arriving in London just after dawn. At this point he was free to do whatever he liked. Such as travelling home.

At some point between clocking on and being disgorged into London, he'd try to remember to find a souvenir for his neighbour. A napkin, a menu card, a shampoo miniature, anything at all so long as it boasted the logo of the famous Caledonian Sleeper, which he would transport all the way back to Portobello, like a migrating bird, in one of his greasy pockets.

"Hahahaha! Mister Bob! Of course you will remember!" said Pavel, "you always remember! Not remember?! Hahaha, I love it, Mister Bob. Very funny, man," and he slid backwards into his flat like a trapdoor spider in reverse.

Mister Bob stood for a moment in silence, heart beating, and then he heard Pavel turn the key in his lock.

Mister Bob sighed, staggered breathlessly down the rest of the stairs, and went outside.

Mister Bob was fat. And he had gingivitis.

Mister Bob closed the front door firmly behind him. Though he closed it firmly, he did not allow it to slam.

His landlady, who lived in one of the flats of the same building, downstairs of his and Pavel's, had chided him several times over slamming the door. He did not want to be on his landlady's shit list. This, alas, was an irrelevant hope because he was already on his landlady's shit list even though he could not recall wronging her. It was not in Mister Bob's nature to miss a rent payment or to make loud noises at night or to bring strange people home or to wilfully damage property or to be rude to anyone. He thought that perhaps, to this landlady, everyone in the world was guilty of every single thing until proven innocent of every single thing and even then there was probably something they were guilty of.

The landlady's somewhat unlikely name was Mrs. Buntapples, but he thought of her as Mrs. Cuntapples. It was just too obviously irresistible. And before you get angry at Mister Bob, you should know that he did not, even in the most secret hiding place of his mind, mean anything sexist or sexual by privately deploying this epithet against her; he meant it purely in the Glaswegian sense.

And even so, he would never knowingly use such an ugly word in the presence of his landlady or that of anyone else, though he suspected in dread that it would slip out sooner or later when he took her his rent cheque. "Yes, ah, Mrs., um, Cuntapples," he would accidentally say, just before being evicted from his home forever.

Door closed, polyester shirt already accumulating a sweaty sheen from the exertions of the staircase, he took the air. It was October now, but it was a warm one. An Indian Summer. Mister Bob preferred the winter, all crisp and unsweaty, which allowed him to stink less badly than usual, but then in the winter he'd fret about slipping on ice and not being immediately able to get back up again and some children coming along and laughing at him or, worse, just silently regarding him.

Although it was unnecessary to have put it on so early in a working day, Mister Bob wore his railway company uniform. He did this because he didn't want to have to carry it around on a coat hanger as if he were returning from the dry cleaners or to have to change his clothes in a cramped toilet cubicle at Inverness. Indeed, there would be little opportunity to change his clothes at Inverness since he would have to go from his commuter train to the station master's office where he would be handed his clipboard to begin checking in the passengers for the sleeper service.

Over his forearm, he carried the North Face overcoat he'd bought from an Aberdeen branch of Millets, the camping shop. It was hot now but experience had taught him that it would be cold on the air-conditioned trains and a jacket designed for weathering the climates of mountain peaks would be just about enough to endure it.

Mister Bob wore his tie short in the way he had done at school more than twenty years ago. Nobody had shown him any other way to wear a tie in the meantime, which a shame because the smallness of the tie gave him an Oliver Hardyesque appearance. It did not, however, draw any particular attention to his stinkiness or his baldness, so it wasn't all bad.

As well as being unseasonably warm, Portobello High Street was oddly still for midafternoon. He imagined that everyone was at the beach, though he did not know why that should be. Mister Bob always felt out of the loop and out of step with what people liked to do. He'd routinely forget about things like bank holidays and school half terms because they were not a part of his world, and he'd turn up to work to find the trains swarming with families and noisy kids, healthy and affluent witnesses to Mister Bob's shame and wretchedness. Perhaps today there was an important town meeting he'd not been aware of because he'd been reading in his book-lined flat or riding an all-stops commuter train to some obscure industrial town in the North of England.

Mister Bob began his walk to the bus stop planted in the tarmac opposite Mike's Fishing Tackle Shop. Officially, this bus stop was called the Portobello Town Hall bus stop, but the town hall was several metres along the road from it. It should really have been called the Mike's Fishing Tackle Shop stop, he mused. And then he felt annoyed that the thought should strike him as novel since he'd had it about seventy or eighty times before.

As one foot fell down in front of the other, a strange series of images came suddenly into Mister Bob's imagination. Perhaps inspired by the sunshine, he imagined first what it would be like to be on holiday in Spain, in a villa he'd found on the Internet, and that he was finally going to try the advertised "plunge pool." The plunge pool was a circular pool with the radius and diameter of a hula hoop, but the depth to Mister Bob was frighteningly unknowable and so he'd avoided it for three days of his holiday. Stinking from not bathing for so long and from sweating in the Alicante sun, he finally vowed to try the plunge pool in order to wash his balls and armpits. It would be refreshing if he could only overcome his fear. Mister Bob lowered himself into the circular aperture of the plunge pool, the water an opaque dark green, almost black, only to find that the pool was deeper than his body was long and that he could not touch the bottom. It would be okay though and he would surely not end up as one of those silly people who died on holiday, their absence unnoticed by work colleagues, who really should have been expecting them back, until weeks later. But then there came a sucking sensation, from some sort of vent deep in the water, and his body was gulped down by the water. As he sank, he consoled himself that at least he wouldn't have to suffer the indignity of being alive any more, but then remembered something he'd read about drowning being a surprisingly painful death, and then, as he descended deeper and deeper by suction device, his lungs filled with stagnant Spanish water, and he died.

You will remember, of course, that none of this actually happened. Mister Bob was not on holiday in Spain and he was neither paused upon the side of a circular plunge pool, seeking the courage to get into it, nor was he being sucked to the deathly bottom. He was in fact on his way to work, walking along the high street of his adopted hometown of Portobello, near Edinburgh in friendly old Scotland. There was nothing to worry about here, other than the sudden and vivid daydreams that fell upon him sometimes. Poor old Mister Bob. How did a daydream with such a long-feeling internal reality occur in the space of a second?

Mister Bob rounded the corner and saw Mike's Fishing Tackle Shop where he used to buy his worms and maggots before Mike filed for bankruptcy due, presumably, to a shortage of people in the world who wanted worms and maggots. The window of the shop was boarded up, a sight that made Mister Bob feel sad and left behind. He crossed the high street to the bus stop down from the town hall and he stood there, waiting, in his earthly form of a 53-year-old man in a polyester railway company uniform with a too-short tie that made him look like Oliver Hardy but balder and, unfortunately, aliver.

I wish I was dead, thought Mister Bob, though he did not actually want to kill himself. Not today anyway. He did not want to kill himself at the present moment, but merely to be dead, maybe to have always been dead. The state of being dead was very appealing to Mister Bob, but the actual dying was not, which is probably why the fear of dying so often featured in his sudden and unasked-for daydreams. He did not want to experience the green water of a holiday plunge pool filling his lungs and he did not want to find out if that book had been correct about drowning being a painful way to go. He just wanted to lie down on the grass and for the earth to reclaim him. He just wanted the vines and the ivy to embrace his knackered old body and to pull him down into the ground, quietly, through the bracken and ferns, through the soft moss and soil and loam, and for it all to be dark and oaky and okay.

The bus was coming, so Mister Bob put out a hand with five small, child-like fingers on it to signal that the bus should stop, which it did.

On the bus, Mister Bob gazed out of the window at nothing in particular. The window of the bus had a discomforting yellowish tinge to it, which made Mister Bob feel queasy.

He had been on this bus, the 124, perhaps two or three hundred times and the windows were always slightly yellowed. It allowed passengers to look upon a parallel universe version of Portobello that consisted largely of stagnant, mucal dripping. Someone like Cormac McCarthy could use that as the inspiration for a miserable dystopian novel. Mister Bob was widely read but he didn't like miserable novels, especially dystopian ones.

The reason Mister Bob did not care for dystopian novels was that he feared people would read them not as warnings but as blueprints. He was concerned that stupid people would read those books about horrible worlds in which young people are hounded through bleak streets for a reality television programme or somesuch and are gunned down before a digital advertising board promoting a commercially-available suicide pill, and find them appealing. Since stupid people inevitably ended up in positions of responsibility, they would imprint this exciting vision, originally conceived by a cultured humanist as the Worst Thing Imaginable, onto real life.

Mister Bob was not a pessimist. He just had strong thoughts sometimes.

The bus pulled into the city centre, the Scott Monument rising into view like something from a spiky Hell. The bus didn't stop very close to the train station so, after alighting with the other passengers, all of whom needed to catch a train, Mister Bob would have to sweat his way from the bus stop to the train station in his polyester railway company uniform with a too-short tie.

Once, when he had made this journey to work on a summer's day with the midday sun high in the August sky and beating down upon his head, Mister Bob had paused to wipe his brow with his pocket railway company handkerchief. As he did so, he was goosed by a jester because the Edinburgh Festival was on.

Now, as he made his way along Prince's Street in October, Mister Bob found himself feeling thankful that there were no jesters around. He thought about that day in August though and it gave him a shudder.

He wondered what it would take to persuade a person to dress up in jingling motley and to goose a struggling man on his way to work. A great deal of unshattered personal confidence, he supposed, and a fine battery of hoarded love.

"A'reet Bob," said David McManaman, the station manager.

"Ah," said Mister Bob, "Hello, um, David."

Though Mister Bob did not feel very confident speaking to the station manager, he had largely positive feelings about him. David was a good egg. He never seemed to be put off by Mister Bob's nervousness or stinkingness or his obvious loneliness. He had never seemed fazed by his too-short tie or his stupid-looking moustache. Few people ever mentioned those things to Mister Bob, of course, but he could tell they were thinking about them. David McManaman was also a bachelor though, and had the red face that comes with decades of alcoholism and also a head in the shape of a triangle, so he probably had his own problems. They had an unspoken sense of tribal loyalty: neither man was a stranger to a Fray Bentos microwaveable pie.

David McManaman wore the same polyester railway company uniform as Mister Bob but David McManaman was better suited to it. David McManaman did not look imprisoned by his uniform or like it had been built around him in the manner of a prefabricated apartment complex. His tie came practically all the way down to his belt buckle too, just as nature intended.

"You'll be arf tae the sneck," said David McManaman. Luckily, Mister Bob could speak his language. "The Sneck" was an alternative name for Inverness, just as "Auld Reekie" was an alternative name for both Edinburgh and Mister Bob.

"You'll be arf tae the sneck."

"Aye," said Mister Bob, "that is, ah, yes, I'm on my way there, um, now."

Mister Bob looked down at his shoes. He'd bought them at Clarks on Argyll Street in Glasgow when he was most recently there for work. He'd had some time to fritter between trains and he'd left the safety of Queen Street Station to wander around and he'd ended up buying these brogues. He'd imagined incorrectly that they'd lend him a dignified or even gentlemanly air but instead, like his tie worn short, they only exaggerated his awkwardness somehow. Still, he'd enjoyed shopping for them and it had allowed him to practise his woeful conversational skills with the shop assistant who had not had a Glasgow brogue at all but a Scouse accent, God love her. Such small encounters, such little freedoms, were something Mister Bob occasionally liked about his job, though they were scant compensation for all the time spent on long-distance journeys like this one from Portobello to Edinburgh to Dunblane to Inverness to London and back again. "Scant compensation" was also a good description of his monthly salary. *Time-wasting, money-grubbing fucking bastards.* The shoes he looked at now were a souvenir of his three-and-a-half hours in Glasgow two weeks ago. He had also eaten some chips there and necked four pints of Tennent's lager if memory served him. And it did. A good memory was one of Mister Bob's assets and it granted him the benefit-cum-curse of a rich inner life.

The shoes did not make him look dignified or gentlemanly. They made him look like a shy, stuffy, portly, prim, old fool. After sinking two of his pints of Tennent's that day in Glasgow, he'd felt emboldened enough to put them on, right there in the Wetherspoons in the middle of the afternoon, and to stash his old shoes in the new Clarks box. For the first time since leaving the shop, he saw the truth of how silly they made him look but through a tipsy two-pint confidence he'd pushed the thought to the back of his mind as if it were the memory of discovering a hair on a looked-forward-to chocolate eclair. He could never get dressing right. He had once seen a picture of a very fat man in a rapping group called Bowling for Soup. That man had looked like a million American dollars in his witty t-shirt and sunglasses and with his tattooed arms. Mister Bob could never find the confidence to buy, let alone wear, a witty t-shirt or sunglasses or a pair of tattooed arms.

Mister Bob could never be a jester or goose a passerby. Mister Bob could never bowl for soup.

When he'd left that rubbishy pub in Glasgow after four pints in the middle of the day, he'd gone into an alleyway near Queen Street Station to be sick. Some of the sick had got onto his new brogues. He'd stooped to clean them with a Pizza Hut napkin he'd found in his polyester railway company uniform jacket pocket and, in doing so, torn the crotch of his trousers. He'd then done the trolley service from Glasgow to Auld Reekie with train carriage air breezing through the tear in the polyester crotch and wondering, half-cut, if he would need to pay for a replacement pair of trousers himself.

"Good-good," said David McManaman positively, "well say a big halloo to yer lass Tracey fer me."

Tracy was Mister Bob's co-worker on the sleeper service from Inverness to London Euston. Their shifts didn't always coincide but the stars had aligned and they were scheduled to work together today.

Tracey was the silver lining of this whole terrible affair. He dearly wanted to know Tracey better than he did but their entire relationship took place at night, half-asleep and sometimes half-drunk, as they were blasted through the Scottish and English countrysides by rail. He sometimes wondered insanely if she would marry him one day if nobody else turned up. It could be like a pact. Mister Bob and Tracey. Mister Bob and Mister Tracey Bob.

"I will that, ah, um, David," said Mister Bob.

I will do no such thing, triangle head, thought Mister Bob, and then felt bad about calling the mild-mannered station manager "triangle head" even though he actually hadn't.

★

A hundred miles an hour. Waterlogged fields, a pheasant, a heron. You knew climate change was a problem when farmers' fields in the Scottish Lowlands were so reliably waterlogged that a heron could live there.

He was on his way to Dunblane now. Dunblane was famous for an incident in the 1990s. A gunman took a sports rifle into a primary school and murdered sixteen children and their teacher in the school gym. It was a terrible, horrible thing and Mister Bob could remember the event viscerally and as if it had only just happened.

Unfortunately, Mister Bob also remembered that some of the parents of the murdered schoolchildren had released a charity record, a cover of the Bob Dylan song, "Knocking on Heaven's Door." It was very catchy.

Now that Mister Bob had remembered the song, he would have to be careful not to absent-mindedly start singing or humming the song in such close proximity to the town in case somebody overheard him and was offended and understandably came at him with a half-brick.

He noticed something strange out in the waterlogged field. A body. It seemed to be the body of a large man with thinning hair, lying motionless and face-down in the water. He was wearing a polyester railway company uniform. Mister Bob ignored it.

Mister Bob had not always lived in Portobello. He had in fact grown up in England. His mother was half-Scottish and, since she had to work after Dad died, young Mister Bob, Master Bob, was all but raised by his "Scotch Gran" on an English council estate.

It was to this world that Mister Bob's mind drifted as the train shot through the green and pleasant abyss. This was another of his tendencies, though perhaps this time it was one shared by most people: a tendency to think of the past when on a long journey. Through rootlessness and boredom and lack of sleep, ghosts are summoned.

Though he had passed many nights in Scotch Gran's pebbledashed semi-detached council house, his memories were largely of the garden, which struck him now as idyllic. He would look for frogs in that garden, migrating from a nearby brook, and he'd often find them too. They were small frogs, about the size of the old five-penny piece. He loved to find a frog and he could watch them for hours. There was also a hole in a privet hedge through which he could squeeze his chubby body and he thought of it as a door of the sort you might find in the garden of a stately home, that might take you into a secret walled garden or a hedge maze. But this was all in a council estate in Little England.

Scotch Gran had many curious little habits, one of which was the saving and hoarding of twenty-pence coins. When she got one in change from buying cigarettes at the corner shop, she would put it into a money box she'd made from a Nescafe instant coffee jar with parchment paper stretched across the top with a slit made in it and secured with a postman-dropped rubber band. She called each coin "a prisoner." She told him that she would "go gambling with them." It struck him as entirely plausible that Scotch Gran was a gambler of twenty-pence pieces though he had no idea where she might do such a thing, never saw her doing it, and never saw the prisoners of the Nescafe instant coffee jar liberated to that end or any other.

Scotch Gran was probably the person he'd inherited his heavy drinking from. Not that it had been a problem for her. But Scotch Gran had had a bewildering range of hard liquor in her cupboard under the sink, a space more traditionally reserved for cleaning supplies and detergents or perhaps a bin. No, under Scotch Gran's sink was a glistening selection of differently shaped booze bottles, the effect of which coincidentally resembled the skyline of Dubai.

Just as these homely reveries began to lull him to sleep, the peace was torn apart by a Boeing 757 driving itself nose-first into the soil of the field, sending a flock of fluffy sheep scattering in all directions.

Philosophers have annoyed people for thousands of years with discussions about "what is real?" How do we know what is real? Is a dream real? Is an imaginary event any less real than one that has happened externally? After all, we generally only experience things inside our heads even if they also happened externally.

Mister Bob sat up suddenly in his chair, heart racing. These things happened sometimes.

There had been no Boeing 757. Not really.

But to Mister Bob there had been.

Sort of.

As he waited for the train to Inverness, Mister Bob found himself singing a little song. "Knock-knock-knockin', on, ah, um, heaven's door..." he sang. Then he realised what he was doing and stopped it immediately.

Lurching and swaying, Mister Bob sat, slouching, on the toilet in the train. Like everyone who'd sat there before him and everyone who would ever sit there after him, he wasn't entirely sure the door was locked.

A padlock symbol was illuminated red, which he took to mean that it was locked. But didn't the colour red indicate danger? A warning that it in fact wasn't locked? He would have felt more confident if he could have tested a door handle, given a real door a real shove to ascertain that a bolt had come down. But it was a futuristic electric door that defied every mammalian sense and could, for all Mister Bob knew, roll open at any moment.

Well, not *any* moment. It would have to be just when Mister Bob was struggling to wipe his bottom, when he was at his most debagged and vulnerable, that the door would inevitably roll open. If it rolled open, he would find himself helplessly shouting "occupied!" while affording the inevitable Mother Superior or party of screaming schoolchildren in the vestibule beyond a glimpse of his browned button, and then have to bear the brunt of their gaze for the full twenty seconds it would take for the door to stutter closed. And that would be if some wag among the observers of his bottom didn't inadvertently (or vertently) press the door-open button again.

None of that happened, thankfully. But it could have done, which was why none of the two poos and six wees Mister Bob required on his commute to Inverness could be conducted in anything approximating comfort.

"Hello there!" said a cheerful voice Mister Bob had heard many times before, "Please do not flush nappies, sanitary products, sandwiches, litter, hopes, dreams, or goldfish down the toilet. Thank you!"

"Fuck, ah, um, off," said Mister Bob.

I mean fuck fucking off, thought Mister Bob.

Mister Bob sat there, hunched like Rodin's most celebrated maquette, thinking of little other than how to respond should the door really roll open and, occasionally, of himself as a tawdry meat sculpture, the railway sleepers drifting away below.

Mister Bob bought a bacon sandwich at the train buffet cart. "Buffet cart" used to strike him as an incongruous term, something quaint from the past. He'd also heard somewhere that the real reason buffet carts still exist on trains were for emergencies; to stop hangry passengers from rioting or resorting to cannibalism during a three-hour delay. But now that he spent so much of his time on trains, it no longer struck him in any way at all. It had become an invisible place, part of the rubbishy ambient background of his days.

For now, at least, the buffet cart was part of his life as a commuter, a passenger, rather than his life as a railway company employee. If he'd been unlucky and known the person on duty in the buffet cart, it might have involved some polite workplace chit-chat and thus transmogrified into a part of his working day but thankfully, having hidden the polyester railway company uniform with his North Face overcoat, he'd been like any other customer, albeit one who looked like he was going skiing. His prize: one bacon butty.

As he sat at his table seat to eat the bacon butty, Mister Bob bit his tongue so hard that it began to bleed.

It bled significantly for a moment and Mister Bob wondered if he hadn't damaged himself irrevocably. There was blood on the bread and blood on the bacon.

When he sipped from the bottle of water he'd bought with the sandwich at the buffet cart, the water stung his tongue where he'd wounded it and a little skein of blood worked its way into the upturned bottle in a skinny red cable.

Mister Bob swallowed his mouthful of bacon butty prematurely and he felt it make an unpleasantly laboured way down his oesophagus. He then stuck his tongue out to examine it in his reflection in the window. The reflection was not good enough to show the tongue in any detail so he would have to wait until his inevitable next bathroom visit to see how badly he had damaged himself. He imagined, however, that what he would see on his tongue would be an angry red swelling.

It crossed Mister Bob's mind that he probably wouldn't have bit his tongue so badly if he weren't an alcoholic.

Mister Bob was what is often described as "a high-functioning alcoholic." He didn't go to any kind of self-help group or concern himself with twelve-step programmes. He just muddled along with it, drinking too much but not usually to the point of annihilation, and trying to accept that being an alcoholic was simply no big deal. So long as he could report to work on time and pay Mrs. Cuntapples her rent on time, he did not see his problem as a problem.

He occasionally saw his problem as a problem in moments like this one, however. If he hadn't been an alcoholic, he mused, he might not be so clumsy and he would not have, for example, ruined his day by biting his tongue while eating a bacon butty from a train buffet cart.

He had once fallen down the escalator to the Euston Tube and made one of his shins bleed quite badly and given himself a headache. An old woman had offered him her stick when it became apparent that he might not be able to stand up again unassisted. But that had been the worst time and it had involved one can of Fosters beer too many from the buffet cart, a mistake he would not make again. He was, after all, high-functioning.

Mister Bob finished the last of his sandwich and tried to ignore the horror of his gory tongue. He picked up his book to read it. Mister Bob had been making his way through the complete works of Stendahl. The book he was reading today was a novel called *Le Rouge et le Noir* or *The Red and the Black* and it chronicled a provincial young man's attempts to socially rise beyond his modest upbringing through a commitment to talent, graft, deception, and hypocrisy. Mister Bob couldn't relate to it at all.

Mister Bob read three pages before he fell asleep and was awoken by a pre-recorded and poorly amplified announcement that his train was arriving into Inverness.

"*Fsst-fuzz-ferst*," said the announcement, "*Invernizz*. Please ensure *foo-fazz-fazz* on alighting from this train. *Kucka-chunk*."

Arriving into Inverness railway station is rarely a special business, except, on this occasion, Mister Bob would get to see Tracey there.

Tracey would give him a nice big smile and say something bawdy, which would make him blush, and then she'd ask what book he'd been reading on the train this time, and then she would say "ooh, fancy" or something along those lines.

Mister Bob was in love with Tracey.

"Hullo Bob!" said Tracey as he passed through the

automated ticket barrier. Tracey was Scottish, originally from Fife, but had moved to Preston some fifteen years ago. As such, her accent had levelled out neatly to something Bordersish, much as Mister Bob's had been tempered by a life in Scotland. Geographically, they'd as good as swapped places. Accent-wise, they'd met in the middle.

"Ah, hello," said Mister Bob, "um, Tracey." His self-mutilated tongue stung as he spoke and, just as he'd feared but not yet seen in a mirror, the entire organ had swollen in his mouth.

He was already blushing and his nose reddened above his moustache. He became suddenly conscious of his too-short railway company necktie, which was visible through the partially-unzipped North Face overcoat. The North Face overcoat had seemed like a stylish and sensible purchase when he was looking at it on the blue-ticket rack in Millets. Now, he felt over-prepared and like someone embarking on the Three Peaks Challenge when, in fact, he was just changing trains at Inverness so he could start his shift.

"How ye diddlin'?" said Tracey and they gave each other a peck on the cheek as any pair of reunited old friends would. There was nothing to it, but then Tracey put out her palm, a little gremlin claw, and briefly cupped Mister Bob's testicles through his polyester railway company trousers.

"Hoo!" said Mister Bob.

"He-*llo*!" said Tracey, laughing.

She could be like this sometimes. A bawdy queen.

Mister Bob's face went as red as his swollen tongue.

That Tracey had voluntarily reached out and touched his genitals, something no woman had done to him in about twenty years, meant nothing to Tracey and almost everything to Mister Bob. It was just the way she was and just the way he was.

Tracey was smiling. She was quite the picture. She had a full set of off-white teeth. She had dyed blonde hair made lank with a hot straightening iron. She wore the same polyester railway company uniform as Mister Bob but, to Mister Bob's eyes, she looked much better than he did in it. She, too, wore the tie a little too short but not as short as Mister Bob did.

"What you readin' today, treasure?" she asked.

"Ah," said Mister Bob, "that would be, um, *Le Rouge et le Noir*." He wouldn't normally use the correct French name if prompted to tell someone what he was reading. He wouldn't normally want to risk the wrath of whomever he was sitting next to on the train, "wot you readin'" essentially being a battlecry in some parts of Britain. "*Le Rouge et le Noir*," no matter how matter-of-factly spoken would have resulted in a whole are-you-some-kind-of-poof conversation he had no desire to get into.

"Ooh!" said Tracey, "Proust?"

"Ah, Stendahl, um, actually," said Mister Bob, still blushing. Tracey had pronounced "Proust" correctly— *proost*, not *prowst*—and that was one of the hints that there was more to this lady than Mister Bob's typical railway company co-worker and part of why he was in love with her. Her correct pronunciation of "Proust" almost suggested that Tracey was rotten by choice. He also liked that they had similar problems in their lives and that her attitude, unlike his, was almost to celebrate and magnify them. Mister Bob felt compromised by his anxieties and dependencies while Tracey seemed practically to thrive on hers. Without her anxieties and dependencies, it seemed to Mister Bob, she would not be whole.

"Ooh! Stendahl," said Tracey in a sort of mock admiration that only partially disguised what Mister Bob thought might be genuine admiration. He'd got one in today. He'd impressed Tracey a little bit. They would all accumulate, these impressions, and in just a century or two if his current trajectory was anything to go by, the two of them would be married and living in a writerly cottage in the Highlands where nobody would bother them and she would gently lap at his smelly genitals with the hungry tenderness of a cat who laps milk, while Mister Bob turned another page of the complete works of Ion Heliade.

"Well, let's get to it... said the actress to the bishop," said Tracey, cackling like a ghoul.

She was not talking about getting married and fleeing to the countryside for a shared life of passionate indulgence. She was talking about clocking in at the station manager's office. Mister Bob had to collect his clipboard for checking the passengers in and Tracey had to collect the drinks' cart for the trolley service. Tracey took Mister Bob's hand and off they went, Mister Bob's stumpy little legs moving quickly to keep up, like the articulated legs of a teddy bear.

As usual, Mister Bob methodically checked each passenger against the names on his clipboard. There was a high-tech self-checking-in machine in the station but passengers either didn't understand it or they didn't notice it, and it didn't work most of the time anyway. He then helped Tracey get the drinks' cart onto the train by opening up the portable wheelchair ramp. He got a blood blister when one of the hinges nipped him. He stowed the ramp away again, cursing it lightly, and, finally, retreated into his cabin for a couple of hours of staring at the wall.

This was the part of the job where he could get his own back. He had travelled to work, off the clock, for hours on end, biting his tongue and not really reading Stendahl properly because of a noxious self-consciousness. But now he would get paid for taking it easy and even for going to sleep while he waited for six carriages of the squawking public to make enough mess from a single evening snack that his one-man cleaning service would be called into action.

In the meantime, Mister Bob was looking forward to removing the railway company uniform for a while. In his sleeping cabin, he stood in front of the little mirror with its creepy rounded corners and the unhomely rivets that fixed it to the bulkhead, to loosen his tie. The tie slid around his neck then hung limp upon his shoulders like a tailor's measuring tape. Mister Bob sighed a sigh of relief and wondered, not for the first time, if it had even been necessary to wear a uniform for so long or at all. Would the passengers really have minded if they'd been checked in by a skivvy in civvies? Would they have even noticed?

A wink from the soap in the soap dish answered his question. It was a small, individually-wrapped soap, circular like a Pontefract Cake. The wrapper boasted the ludicrously proud "Monarch of the Glen" emblem of the Caledonian Sleeper. The passengers of this particular train liked a certain kind of old-fashioned verisimilitude, and that's why he had to wear a uniform. The hour or so he spent checking passengers in with a clipboard was part of the illusion that they were boarding the Orient Express or something. It was the sort of thing Pavel would enjoy as a train enthusiast and, as was more common among the passengers on the train, the sort of thing expected by an oil-drilling slimebag travelling between Aberdeen and London with a keen eye for getting the most out of an expense account.

As Mister Bob unfastened the top button of his polyester railway company uniform, there came a knock at the door. Passengers didn't usually seek him out after he'd come into his cabin and almost none of them knew where he would be hiding anyway. It would have to be the train manager, who, along with all managerial types, was a class traitor practically by definition. Mister Bob held his breath and considered the merits of not responding to the knock.

"Come off it Bob," came the voice behind the door, "I can see the light on."

It was Tracey. Tracey!

Mister Bob opened the door. Opening the door of a sleeper train berth had the sensation of opening a kitchen cabinet. What was inside the kitchen cabinet of this particular bachelor, however, was not a haphazard mixture of poorly-scrubbed pots and a grubby colander, but a woman—a woman who was also one of his favourite people in the world—brandishing a six-pack of premium strength lager.

"Happy Birthday, Big Bob," said Tracey, flashing Mister Bob a wide and off-white smile.

"Thank you!" said Mister Bob, "But, ah, it isn't, um, my birthday."

In the cosmic gap between "ah" and "um," Mister Bob's fast and routinely overstimulated mind considered going along with the confusion and accepting that it was his birthday. In the end, before the "um," he had decided that honesty was the best policy.

"Oh," said Tracey, "Isn't it? Shall I take these home then?"

She waggled the six-pack in a practised gesture like a ventriloquist with her hand inside a puppet head.

"Not at all, not at all," said Mister Bob and gestured warmly into the private cabin. It was in fact a bunk room and the only way for two people to sit down was for both of them to clamber into the bottom bunk and to sit cross-legged and facing each other like a pair of Yogis in a business meeting. So this is what Tracey and Mister Bob did. As Tracey crawled onto the bottom bunk, she pointed her boney and polyester railway company uniform-clad bottom in Mister Bob's direction. He tried not to leer and he wondered if she was already drunk, had in fact been drunk before he'd even met her at Inverness.

Suddenly, taking leave of his senses and acting entirely out of character, Mister Bob grasped Tracey's trousers at the waistband, pulled them violently down about her ankles and buried his face in the cleft of her exposed bottom. Her buttocks were pimpled and there was what looked like a healed cigarette burn on her thigh. The smell of her bum was a combination, a potpourri, of Mum-brand deodorant, carbolic soap and a playful hint of poo. "*Yeah*," said Mister Bob, with a note of evil.

This didn't happen. It was another of Mister Bob's visions like the plunge pool episode and the aeroplane disaster that had felt almost completely real. This vision, like the others, had been an unwelcome one. A deeply unwelcome one. The worst thing had been the details his imagination had concocted without his say-so. Her scent. The cigarette burn. He didn't know where it could all have come from.

Mister Bob shook his head a little in a "snap out of it" way to find Tracey proffering a can of lager in his direction.

Smiling benignly and trying to tamp his vision back into the swamp of his preconscious mind, he meekly accepted the can and clambered into the bunk bed.

"Who, ah, is the, um, train manager this evening?" asked Mister Bob as a way of regrounding things, making his world once again stable and trivial.

"It's Sunny," said Tracey.

"Ah," said Mister Bob, "that, um, gobshite."

"Yup," said Tracey, "another night of bullshit for the likes of us to guzzle down."

Sunny wasn't the worst train manager Tracey and Mister Bob had ever worked with but he was an exceptional nuisance nonetheless. The problem was that he was a pole climber and he had a particularly officious, self-important way of barking orders. His angry, uptight nature contrasted with his dopey Midlands accent, though the juxtaposition didn't quite serve to take the edge off his generalised cuntery.

Tracey expertly cracked open her premium strength lager using only one hand. It fizzed up and some of the yellowish foam fuzzed down onto the bunk's topsheet.

"Whoops!" said Tracey, "nobody sleeping here tonight, I hope?" and she flashed him a wink and a bit of green tongue. He laughed politely.

Mister Bob more gracefully opened his own can of premium strength lager. He was more than capable of opening it one-handed as Tracey had done, he being all too familiar with the practice of boozing in one's sleeping quarters, but he wanted to maintain a sense of decorum. He was, after all, in love with Tracey and he wanted to impress her.

Mister Bob took a swig of the premium strength lager, and the familiar dirty-water flavour made him feel more like his authentic self again. While he was drinking, he would not be subject to nightmarish visions, would not be under the cosh of his job somehow. Even though he was technically working now, he was cheating the system, occupying a halfway state between toil and freedom.

He sipped his premium strength lager again, almost coquettishly, like how a dainty fairy princess would drink her premium strength lager. Decorum. On the other hand, he didn't want Tracey to feel uncomfortable or that she couldn't relax or act without restraint. To counter his acts of prissiness, he burped.

"*Baarp*," said Mister Bob. A burp was one pronouncement he could manage without an "ah" or an "um."

"Steady on," said Tracey. She adjusted her position from the Yoga squat, opening her legs and leaning on one knee. Once again, Mister Bob was quietly surprised by her bold way of exposing her vulnerable areas to him.

A small man roughly the size of an Action Man or Barbie doll appeared between Tracey's polyester-clad thighs. He was moving in a slightly clunky and unreal way, like a special effect in an old Ray Harryhausen science-fiction film. It was the first time Mister Bob could recall one of his waking nightmares seeming at all unreal and not, as it usually went, realer than real.

The little man was wearing a high-vis *gilet* and noise-cancelling headphones and he gestured emphatically between Tracey's legs with a pair of luminous rods. He was an airport runway worker waving Mister Bob in.

Don't look at him, Mister Bob told himself silently, scrunching his eyes and gritting his teeth, *he's not real.*

And, sure enough, when Mister Bob opened his eyes again, the little man had vanished.

The little man might have had a point though. Was Tracey waving Mister Bob in? Or was she, on some level, thinking of waving him in later in the evening? She had, after all, come to his cabin at the first available opportunity this evening, brandishing a six-pack of premium strength lager, which she had presumably bought in advance and planned to bring to him, on the entirely transparent pretence that she thought it was Mister Bob's birthday when it was not. Would he be able to kiss her? Now he really wished he hadn't chomped his tongue so badly. It all seemed too unlikely to him. It was more likely, he reasoned, that Tracey saw him as such an unsexual person that she wouldn't think twice about flirting with him, goosing him, or sitting with him on what was, albeit only temporarily, his bed. There was no way a man like Mister Bob would make any kind of move on her. That's probably what she was thinking. That or she thought Mister Bob, with his *Le Rouge et le Noir*, was gay.

"Ah," said Mister Bob with even more awkwardness than usual, "I'm not, um, gay, you know?"

"I know," said Tracey, and she belched. It was a particularly revolting belch from the side of her mouth, the oral equivalent of a left-cheek sneak, but Mister Bob found it perfectly charming.

"You're an eligible bachelor," said Tracey, "not a confirmed one."

Mister Bob was impressed. "Confirmed bachelor" was an old, almost Victorian, euphemism for homosexual and it was nice that she knew it. He wondered if she had read any Wilde. Plus the way she'd skilfully said "eligible" without stammering or adding extra b's while in her current state of inebriation was cute. Mister Bob smiled.

"You just need a bath is all," said Tracey, "because, sometimes, you fucking reek."

Mister Bob sputtered. Some premium strength lager came out of his nose.

"Ah," said Mister, "a, um, a bath?"

"Yeah," said Tracey, "you know, rub-a-dub-dub?" and she made a scrubbing-her-back motion followed by a sarcastic, almost monkey-like, washing under the arms gesture.

Mister Bob sighed. Tracey sometimes used insults as a way of being perverse, as a way of almost flirting with him, as a way of injecting energy and naughtiness into staid workplace chit-chat. She'd referred in the past to his weight while patting his belly, to his moustache ("hello, Tom Selleck!"), and to the thinning hair on the top of his head by inexplicably walking her fingers through it and saying "cuckoo! cuckoo!", but never before had she made reference to Mister Bob being smelly. It cut close to the bone and it made Mister Bob feel suddenly very sad. If he'd had an erection, it would have shrivelled. But he didn't have an erection so there was nothing to shrivel, and this made Mister Bob feel sad as well.

"You should pay special attention to your arse crack," she said, "and your taint."

Mister Bob didn't know what a taint was and he didn't ask.

"Oh," he said instead, "I didn't know that," and he took a crumpled, non-decorum-hampered swig of his beer.

Tracey saw that she had hurt him and her response was not to apologise (for this was not in her nature) but to unfurl and extend the leg she'd been leaning on and to kick him, hard, in the shoulder, cackling.

"Drink your beer," she said.

Mister Bob quickly got over his woundedness. Between them, Tracey and Mister Bob finished the six-pack, talking away a goodly part of the night.

He savoured these moments with Tracey and committed them importantly to a bank of treasured memories. Once, he remembered fondly, he and Tracey had been skiving in an empty First Class carriage, making headway into a gigantic plastic bottle of White Lightning. A well-dressed commuter had looked in, seen them, and promptly gone back to

Standard. "Maybe she didn't have a First Class ticket," he'd said but he knew in his heart that the woman had correctly assessed their mild on-duty drunkenness and wanted no part of it. "Or maybe," Tracey had said, "she saw that look in your eye." "What look?" Mister Bob had asked. "The look that says you wanted to rub your grubby little dick all over her perfect lavender-scented tits." This was the sort of bawdy queen business you got from Tracey sometimes. And she hadn't even been that drunk.

There came a bang at the door and Mister Bob extracted himself from his coiled-up position in front of Tracey on the lower bunk. The private cabin struck him for the first time that evening as chilly. The door-banger banged again.

"Ah," said Mister Bob, "just, um, coming."

He fastened the top buttons of his polyester railway company shirt for decorum's sake but there was no time, Mister Bob felt, to tie the tie. Besides, it was late now and he was within his rights not to be wearing a tie, he felt. He might be on the clock but the company assumed he'd be resting until the time came for a cleaning run.

Mister Bob opened the door, that funny little kitchen cabinet feeling, to the train's night manager.

Sunny looked furious, really just a fire axe away from violent mania. Though younger than Mister Bob by at least a decade, Sunny had a way of making Mister Bob feel exceptionally chided and small. Sunny was trim, had an impressive but tidy beard and very neat, side-parted hair. And yet he was not a vision of total perfection; Sunny had bloodshot eyes and some interesting pockmarks above the beard on his left cheek. It looked as if he'd been blasted with shrapnel from a landmine. Or maybe they were chickenpox scars. But Sunny didn't strike Mister Bob as a pock picker somehow.

Sunny's largely-pulled-togetherness evidently paid dividends because, even though Sunny was an utter bastard, he'd been married, Mister Bob knew, for over ten years. He co-owned with his wife a detached house next to a BP petrol station, which must have been convenient for both petrol and midnight snacks.

"*Robert*," Sunny snapped, "there's a blocked toy-lit in Coach D. It's overflowin' and there ay no toy-lit paper and there's shit everywhere. Fock knows where Tracey's got to but she ay no where she's supposed to be..."

Mister Bob immediately bristled. Tracey was where she wanted to be, which, so far as he was concerned, was the only place she was "supposed to be." *Why don't you go and sit in your poxy Renault Espace*, thought Mister Bob, *only don't forget to attach a hose to the exhaust pipe and pop it through the driver's side window while you're in there.*

"...sort it out for me wud ya, Robert. Y'know where the equipment is."

Ah yes, thought Mister Bob, *the equipment. The excellent-quality equipment provided by the railway company for unblocking toilets. The truly top-drawer and considerate-of-user equipment that always leaves you unscathed and not at all drenched in chemicals and urine. The equipment we'd been trained to use by someone who had not only seen the equipment at least once before but used it in battle conditions.*

"Ah," said Mister Bob, "yes, um, Sunny, I will sort that out. Just let me, ah, get my, um, shoes on. Coach, ah, um, D."

Thankfully, instead of waiting around while Bob scrambled for his unfashionable shoes and his railway company tie, Sunny stormed off down the corridor. Mister Bob hadn't wanted to give away Tracey's whereabouts, which, as it happened, were directly behind the door of his private cabin with her hand over her mouth and surrounded by crumpled beer cans. He closed the door and bolted it.

"Thanks Bob," said Tracey, "And don't worry about the backed-up bog, I'll sort it out."

Tracey scrambled out of the lower bunk and got up onto her feet. She began to look around for her shoes, which didn't take long since the entire floor was not much bigger than a single square metre.

"Catch you on the flip side," said Tracey, "and think about what I said."

She said the latter part with a tone of significance, gave him a kiss on the cheek, unbolted the door, and stepped out into the corridor, closing it tightly behind her.

Mister Bob turned around and looked out of the window for a minute at the darkened countryside. The industrious blades of wind turbines gave the effect of marching giants.

Think about what she said, thought Mister Bob. It could only have been about his reeking, about his need for a bath. What a terrible thing to have to hear from someone you liked. Was she saying though, in essence, that she might be interested in him if only he weren't so smelly? Was she saying she might be romantically interested in Mister Bob, that she could overlook his thinning hair and his rubbishy dress sense if only he could stop being smelly? He wasn't completely certain. Mister Bob liked to read but he wasn't always so good at reading between the lines.

Mister Bob contemplated what he would do next. Now that Tracey was out of the picture, it would no doubt involve giving the full length of the train a once-over for coffee cups and other rubbish before holing up on the top bunk of his cabin, knocking back two of the whiskey miniatures he'd brought along in his travel bag, and some lonely wanking as he watched the wind turbines and farmhouses pass listlessly by in the night. Sleep would inevitably come and he'd probably fall into an anxious dream about something exciting like slow water ingress.

Mister Bob shivered and took his unfashionably old mobile phone out of his polyester railway company trouser pocket to check the time.

23:49, it said, 17 October.

Oh, thought Mister Bob, *it actually is my birthday*.

54 today.

Two

There were two things that daunted Mister Bob about the bathtub. The first was that, since he'd never actually filled it with water, he wasn't completely certain that the floor would hold the weight.

On the one hand, the bathtub had been installed, presumably, by professionals who knew what they were doing. On the other, the building was a hundred and twenty years old and the floors didn't seem particularly sturdy. Maybe they were rotten. Maybe the building hadn't been built with water-filled bathtubs in mind. Didn't the floor of Mister Bob's bedroom dip in the middle? If he filled the tub today, it struck Mister Bob as entirely plausible that it, and he with it, could smash through the floor, through Pavel's flat, through Mrs. Cuntapples' living room, through the basement, into the sewers, and so on and so on all the way through to Australia.

The other thing that daunted him about the bathtub was that he might not fit in it.

But he must try. He had decided to try.

The hot tap complained with a squeak as Mister Bob turned it.

Water gushed forth.

The water that gushed forth from the hot tap was not exactly hot. It took quite a while to reach a temperature that anyone would generously describe as "hot" and, when it did, it became cool again quite quickly.

This wouldn't do. But the bathtub required a certain volume of water as well as a certain temperature so Mister Bob accepted that some cold or tepid water in the mix was still useful.

He would have to look at the boiler. He strode purposefully out of the bathroom and opened the hall closet. He pulled it open against a certain resistance from the mountains of unopened manila envelopes and Domino's Pizza menus and gate-fold special offer pamphlets from Farmfoods ("Oven chips for a quid! The ideal weeknight dinner for the useless, stinking singleton! Only at Farmfoods!") that shamefully, through procrastination and triage, flooded the hall floor after they'd drifted in, day after day, through the letterbox.

Inside, the boiler hummed in a way he hadn't heard before. It didn't exactly *sound* like a tired man ascending a flight of stairs but it had precisely the same attitude of struggle and Mister Bob recognised it straight away. Alas, this was no time for sympathy and Mister Bob thumped the side of the boiler unit with a heavy wet fist.

The boiler groaned.

Mister Bob tapped the dial. He didn't know what the dial was for. Its little plastic needle was pointing to the left, to a nine o'clock red zone. That didn't seem like a good thing.

Something in the back of Mister Bob's memory, a deep and almost reptoid memory snagged somewhere along his spinal cord, told Mister Bob that this was about "boiler pressure." Mister Bob did not know who had educated him about boiler pressure, if indeed that's what this was about, and under what circumstances the lesson had happened. It was probably some sanctimonious, working-class hero who had clambered so many feet onto a high horse as to necessitate an oxygen tank.

There was a little tap on the boiler that looked like it would help things if he turned it. On the other hand, it might issue forth a high-pressure jet of scalding steam like something dreamed up by Wallace and Gromit's evil twins, that would relieve him of face meat forever.

Mister Bob decided to leave the boiler alone.

As he made his way back to the bathroom, wondering if his single thump to the side of the boiler's unintelligent casing had been efficacious despite the dismal read-out on the dial, one of the Farmfoods leaflets caught his eye. Oven chips. Pizza. Smiley potato faces. He should just get something rubbish out of the freezer, whack it in the oven, and forget all about this bath and boiler business. The happy old sofa and a good book would have him back, unconditionally.

No. It was bathtime. He must try.

He checked the dismally shallow water in the bath. Cold.

He checked the water that was gushing forth from the so-called hot tap. Cold.

Mister Bob knew of only one other way to make hot water. There was only one thing for it. He'd have to act like a Roman slave and fill the Emperor's tub with buckets of hot water.

Mister Bob went to the kitchen and filled the kettle.

Mister Bob boiled six kettles of water, filling the kettle to the line marked "MAX" each time, and added their steaming contents to the bathtub, which continued to fill from the taps with tepid water. He found that it was working fairly well—that the heat provided by the kettle water and the volume provided by the gushing bath taps—was going to be enough. It was certainly hard work to walk back and forth between the kitchen and the bathroom with kettles of boiled water though.

The bathroom filled pleasantly with steam. Mister Bob inhaled the steam through his nostrils and out through his mouth.

He thought about the public baths of Ancient Rome. Mosaics. Different pools and tubs for different temperatures of water and different treatments. How was it that the Ancient world could be so refined and luxurious but today's world was so meagre and dim by comparison. Was this progress? He was doing his best to create an atmosphere of luxury but it was all so basic, so sordid, and such hard work to get to even a baseline level of relaxation. The modern world, it struck Mister Bob not for the first time but perhaps for the first time with such clarity of example, was also a very lonely place. The bath houses of Rome were a communal, social affair. Today's bathing experience was inherently solitary. People sat like private islands in their tepid, lonely ponds.

In a rare contrast to his usual nightmare visions, he imagined that he could one day—once he'd become good at this bathing business—convince someone to join him so they could relieve each other of their loneliness? Perhaps Tracey could come over and they could scrub each other's backs with coarse brushes capable of flaying the old dead skin and the old dead stress, laughing with delight and unencumbered by polyester railway company uniforms.

Probably not, thought Mister Bob.

But maybe! Who knew? There were all sorts of people out there with all sorts of predilections and values and designs on life. If not lovely Tracey, then perhaps he could convince *someone* to join him in the rub-a-dub-dub of the tub-a-lub-dub.

But he was getting ahead of himself. The steam was rising and filling the bathroom but the bathtub itself was nowhere near ready. He estimated that he'd need the surface of the water to rise by at least another two inches to get the over-the-shoulder coverage he was hoping for. And he had no idea of the temperature and would doubtless need to boil one more kettle.

He put his hand into the water to test the temperature, remembering too late that you were supposed to check the temperature with the elbow and not the hand. Or was that a way to test the temperature of milk for babies? He couldn't remember. There was so much information about the world and about life which Mister Bob had pushed to the back of his mind, to the vault of information deemed superfluous to his job with the railway company.

At any rate, the water seemed to his hand to be a perfectly nice temperature for a bath. And the water was still gushing forth from the taps so he would get the volume he needed soon enough.

Would he get in?

He would.

Was it time to get into the bathtub?

It was.

Okay, then. Mister Bob would get into his first bath in almost fifty years. It was a momentous occasion. *Here*, thought Mister Bob through the continuing sound of the gushing tap water, *goes nothing*.

He leaned forward and held onto one of the silver handles, putting his weight down on it. He then realised that no matter how much weight he transferred to the handle, he still struggled to get his first leg high enough to step over the side of the bathtub. God, he was tired.

This hadn't been a problem when he was a boy. When he was very small, his mother or Scotch Gran, whoever had the time that day, would lift him and pop him into the water like a tower crane delivering a partition wall to a new office building, Baby Bob beaming with delight. When he was a little older, he could get his own leg over. Into the bathtub, that was. Now, today, he was too clapped out to get his leg over. Into the bathtub, that was. Or indeed anything else, he imagined.

His legs seemed so small, almost like the legs of a baby. They were chubby, infantile.

He tried again, this time successfully, by swinging a leg energetically over the side of the bathtub, his foot landing in the water with a bathtubby *thunk*.

Yow!

"Fuck," said Mister Bob.

The water was *far* too hot. How? *How* could the water be too hot? He had tested it with his hand!

Mister Bob reflected that foot and hand skin were evidently made of different types of body material.

The water was scorching.

No, the water was *scalding*. That was the word his mother had always used when checking the temperature of his childhood baths. "If it's too hot," she'd said, "you'll be scalded."

She was so dramatic, his mother. So severe. The image that had come to mind whenever she'd said "scalded" was of his own little skeleton, blackened, in the bottom of the tub. It came back to him now. The vision of his now-larger skeleton, charred like coal, flickered electric before his eyes like a warning sign.

Somehow, despite having one foot still on the dry bathroom floor, he lifted his pink and babyish leg out of the too-hot water and held it aloft, dripping. He felt the muscles and tendons between his legs and in his lower back, muscles he hadn't heard from in a very long time, complaining bitterly.

"Okay," said Mister Bob, "duly noted," in response to the muscles' complaints about being treated so badly.

On that, Mister Bob slipped. He lunged forward and fell, bodily, into the bathtub. He was on all fours, hands and feet and knees and shins submerged. The water came up to his elbows and halfway above his knees. Stranded like this, he must have looked like a half-grapefruit in a cup.

The bathwater did not feel too hot on his hands, arms, or legs. It still felt hot to his feet though he always did have cold feet. He wondered if there was any cure for cold feet. If he ever succeeded in sharing a bed with another person again it would be nice not to shock them with his ice cold feet.

He may have been 54 years old and he might have been cursed with cold feet, but now that he had succeeded in running a bath—and, by hook or by crook, actually getting into it—he would no longer be smelly and, as such, may not be alone forever.

One thing at a time, thought Mister Bob.

His penis bobbed on the water like a fishing float.

He wasn't used to seeing it like this. It had a forlorn, castaway attitude. It listed to one side like a dead sea animal. He looked at the small, stalk-like growth growing on its tip, protruding at an angle like a crab's eye. It was exactly the sort of thing you were supposed to see a doctor about but it had been there for long enough now, resident through putting it off and putting it off, that it was evidently harmless. It was practically a part of him. Taking it to a doctor now would be like taking the problem of having an arm or a leg or a foot to a doctor. Pointless. It wasn't as if he was completely averse to dying anyway.

Going to the doctor on a schedule like Mister Bob's seemed like a pipedream. It would be a truly unachievable luxury. Mister Bob had to work. And when he wasn't working, he had to travel to work or else recover from work or else muffle the blow of this violently tedious regimen by drinking heavily. That all took time and energy. He didn't even have time or energy to cook a decent meal save for some Farmfoods potato smiley faces or a Fray Bentos microwavable pie and, until now, hadn't found the time for a bath. He'd still washed, of course, with tepid water from the small Victorian wash basin but evidently, as Tracey had so delicately explained to him, it wasn't enough. Nothing was enough. He worked and worked but he never had anything. Not money. Not dignity. Not even the time of his own life.

Mister Bob's penis, floating and limp, along with its crab's eye, was too depressing to contemplate so he sought out an ancient flannel from the little tiled shelf at the foot of the tub to cover himself with. At first the flannel resisted; crusty and dusty, it had frozen into the shape (and had the general menacing demeanour) of one of Louise Bourgeois' "Mother" sculptures. But it soon relented. The flannel was pink and once it was soaked through with bathwater and covering his penis, it adopted a less arachnoid appearance and took on the friendlier personality of an octopus. Mister Bob had once read in the newspaper about an octopus that had escaped its tank in an aquarium—it was at a tourist attraction somewhere like Canada or New Zealand—and squelched off down the street and back into the ocean. He assumed that his octopus-like flannel would not make a similar bid for freedom, taking his penis along for the ride, but one never knew.

He thought back to the last time he'd taken a bath. It must have been in childhood. He did not recall musing about his penis in such a way in childhood or noticing that it bobbed on the water like a little fishing float. He did not recall the urge in childhood to cover himself with a flannel, inadvertently creating an octopus.

"Hmm," said Mister Bob. His voice sounded strange in the sonic environment of the filled bathtub.

It wasn't quite an echo like one would hear in a tunnel or a large empty room but it was muted, sonorous.

It was all coming back to him. Mister Bob's senses were alive in a new way.

"Hmm," said Mister Bob again, "hum-hum. Haaaaaah-hum."

The quality of the sound took him back in time. Mister Bob began to relax backwards into the hot water and he closed his eyes.

The hot water tickled his armpits and finally claimed his shoulders, which resulted in a noteworthy change in consciousness. He remembered Scotch Gran telling him that so long as your shoulders are covered—with warm water, with a scarf, with bedclothes—you will feel warm. His grandmother had been correct.

His skin stuck slightly—no, it did not *stick* but *rumbled* against—the sides of the bathtub. All of these sensations were things he could remember from long ago but had not thought about in decades.

He remembered bubble bath. Bubble bath! He had not thought about bubble bath for years and years and years. He could remember the smell. He must buy some bubble bath for next time.

Next time. Yes, Mister Bob would do this again. He had only been in the bathtub for fifty, perhaps seventy, seconds and it was already worth the hassle of boiling six kettles.

Hairs and bits of fluff and other less identifiable fragments floated on the surface of the water. He should have cleaned the tub before filling it. And next time, yes *next time*, he would. He would do better with his baths. He would do better more generally.

Bubble bath, he supposed, would take care of the hairs and other floating things too. He wouldn't have to look at them. Nor would he have to cover his fishing float with a dirty old flannel if it were obscured with fluffy white bubbles.

Bubble Bath. His bubble bath when he was a boy had come in a plastic bottle with a smiley face on it and... a hat? Yes, a hat! The bottle in which the bubble bath had come was in the shape of a little sailor man. The plastic cap of the bottle had had the form of a white sailor hat and the bottle itself had had a friendly face and a stripey, nautical shirt printed onto it. Mister Matey! The sailor, that is the gimmick and the brand of the bubble bath, had been called "Mister Matey"— as in "avast, ye matey," he supposed—and he hadn't thought about Mister Matey in over forty years. How had he forgotten so completely about his jolly old bathtime friend?

And there had been other friends too, hadn't there? A family of three rubber ducks... no, hollow plastic ducks, and a rubbery jellyfish thing with googly eyes, and a wind-up frog (he'd called it "Froggo") and...

Mister Bob felt himself relaxing for the first time in a long time. It might have been the first time he had relaxed, *properly* relaxed, in his entire, horrible life. Thank goodness Tracey had been so rude to him. She was a wise one, that Tracey Balfour.

Relaxing. What an option. Relaxing and...

Mister Bob heard a sound. A creaking, groaning sound. An almost *architectural* sound.

It wasn't any sound he recognised from experience but it was one that inspired fear. Beams buckling? Wetted wood splintering? He opened his eyes wide as the bathroom shot through the ceiling or, perhaps, the bathtub fell through the floor.

"*Mister Bob!*" shrieked Pavel.

Mister Bob awoke with a jolt and bumped his coccyx on the bottom of the bathtub.

The bathtub had not fallen through the floor.It was resting upon at least a foot's worth of structural concrete and another six inches of what Victorian builders called "deafening," a compound of ash and crushed seashells intended to minimise noise between the floors of tenement buildings. Mister Bob was as safe as could be and had merely nodded off briefly into another micro-nightmare.

Mister Bob was not, as you might imagine, a narcoleptic. He was a damaged soul, worry-worn by life, blasted and tired. He had pushed this self knowledge momentarily to the back of his mind and the way it had chosen to rush back to the front of his mind again was a blinding moment of super-real horror.

The moment had lasted no more than one second of time but it had hit the comprehension centre of his brain in astonishingly high definition. He had heard the groaning of floorboards, he had felt the sensation of falling, he had tasted the limey flavour of concrete dust as it hung—or had seemed to hang—in the air. The moisture of the steam rising from the hot bathwater had not gone away and had in fact seemed to carry the smell of old masonic dust. He had glimpsed the jagged shapes of fanged, wrecked floorboards, got the sense of hob nails and screws in chaos, seen the panicked eyes of his neighbour, and even touched a future moment of a thousand historic railway timetables falling and fluttering and settling like those million A4 sheets of office paper had done on 9/11 but all in a single room. Mister Bob had *felt* the fall. His arse had absorbed the full shock of the bathtub hitting Pavel's floor and then the shock had reverberated up his spine like a lightning rod but in reverse.

His arse had absorbed no such thing.

There had been no fall. No fall, no landing.

Except, in a way, it really had. And there had been. And there had.

While Mister Bob's mind rejoined his body and returned him to the peace of the steamy bathroom, something in him still reeled from a very distressing incident.

Poor old Mister Bob.

Heart racing and lungs struggling to draw enough oxygen against the weight of the bathwater and the hot steam which still hung in the air, Mister Bob wondered if he could ever afford to relax again.

He had relaxed, remembered such treasures from

boyhood as his old friend Mister Matey the bubble bath sailor man, only to nod off briefly and to experience trauma.

What's wrong with me? wondered Mister Bob. *Is this how other people live?*

There came an urgent banging at the door.

"Mister Bob! Mister Bob!"

Mister Bob, water dripping slightly from the roll of fat behind his skull and down the back of his neck, opened the door to Pavel, worrying that maybe something really had gone wrong and that bathwater was running into Pavel's flat or something.

"Mister Bob, I heared noises."

Pavel pronounced "heard" as "heared," which Mister Bob suddenly found strangely endearing. It helped him to shrug off the frustration of his ruined bathtime, of having it interrupted first by a terror vision and again by a banging at the door.

Mister Bob had managed to get into his bathrobe before answering the door and before Pavel could bash it in. Before today, the bathrobe had been merely a dressing gown for when Mister Bob had a rare few hours to himself and was able to flop around his flat like a sea lion.

But today it really was a bathrobe and when he answered the door in it with wet hair, he thought Pavel would read between these complicated lines and understand what the noises had been.

"I heared noises, Mister Bob," said Pavel again.

"Yes," said Mister Bob, "that would have been my bath."

"Bath, Mister Bob?"

"Yes Pavel, I have been taking a bath."

Pavel looked confused. It was understandable. Mister Bob had lived above Pavel for years and he had never taken a bath in all that time. The pipes must have been groaning with surprise and the floorboards must have been creaking in alarm and Pavel must have wondered what it was all in aid of, not to mention the bump he probably heard when Mister Bob had clumsily fallen over the side and into the bathtub.

Mister Bob explained a little further about how, sometimes, it was nice for even a single man such as himself to indulge in a luxurious bath, so as to become ever-so-slightly less stinky, to slough off a day's or week's or, okay, thirty years' worth of despair and grot.

After a few minutes of pontificating about stinklessness as a positive virtue and enthusing about the joys of hot water and how modern life wasn't conducive to slow-moving luxurious experiences (much less social ones) and how bubble bath and bath toys and other memories of childhood bathtimes had come back to him with a simple adjustment of state memory, it occurred to Mister Bob that, for the entire duration of this conversation, he had not said the words "ah" or "um."

November

Three

Mister Bob was in London again after one of his monster commutes from Portobello to Inverness and one of his not-unmonstrous work shifts on the sleeper train. He had not been working with Tracey on this occasion and nobody had come to bang on the little kitchen cupboard-like entrance to his sleeping cabin. In fact, he'd found himself hiding in there before the train had even left Inverness. A crowd of oddly polite protesters from Extinction Rebellion had glued themselves to the roof of the train and it had taken a couple of hours for the Highlands plod to unstick them.

This was all fine by Mister Bob. In hiding, he'd been able to read undisturbed—the first volume of *Don Quixote* this time, which was good but, Mister Bob felt, needlessly scatological and with a tendency to dwell on romantic-minded but ultimately grotesque individuals—and to get quietly drunk on his own. By the time they got moving again, he fell mercifully to sleep in the bottom bunk, which was the one he preferred to sleep in, the distance up to the top bunk being tricky for a man with short legs to vault; but not before watching the silently marching giants beyond the window pane that were in reality wind turbines.

He now stood, in full polyester railway company regalia (regalia!), upon the concrete concourse outside Euston Station. Often, Mister Bob would hurry-and-lunge straight onto the next available train to Waverley, but today he had some important business in London.

Mister Bob surveyed the concrete crapness of the station's environs. There were some moneyed-looking English types standing around with their hands in their pockets and laughing fatuously. There were also some young people walking along with some sort of take-away stew in paper containers not unlike popcorn buckets. Though they came with a throw-away plastic spoon sticking out of them like an antenna, the young people seemed content just to drink from the bucket as if it were a cup. He'd noticed this the last time he'd been to Euston; a fashion for eating lumpy slop from paper buckets. London! The Great Metropolis! The Centre of the World! Eating lumpy slop from paper buckets did not strike Mister Bob as particularly sophisticated or dignified. But then he remembered who he was. He was Mister Bob. And he, himself, was not particularly sophisticated or dignified either. He was not above eating lumpy slop from a paper bucket. He was, lest we forget, a crap-moustached loner and, in addition to his gingivitis, he was starting to suspect he had athlete's foot. He'd caught himself splaying his toes inside his shoe and rubbing them against the inside of the sock to try and stop the itch.

Mister Bob hadn't thought about athlete's foot since the 1980s. He'd assumed that athlete's foot had gone extinct. He wondered if he should tell someone about this miracle return from the brink. If athlete's foot could survive extinction, maybe the humpback whale and the kakapo and even humanity could survive too.

Mister Bob kicked his way through the pigeons and the discarded slop buckets that were rolling around his feet forlornly and made his way to Babish.

"Babish" was the name of a newsagent and general store near to Euston Station. It was where Mister Bob went if he ever needed of food or other essentials on his brief stops in London. It did not require him to stray far from the station and, as such, he could usually get what he needed without missing the next Edinburgh train.

BABISH, read the sign above Babish's shop window. It was spelled out in a somehow civic-minded font with rounded edges and in an unmistakably 1970s orange colour. Also on the sign and beneath the name of the shop, an imitation of cursive script read, "the everything shop."

The proprietor of BABISH, the everything shop, was a man called Babish. Mister Bob would have liked to have thought of Babish the man as a reliable old companion to whom he could turn when he needed him —a Hastings to his Poirot, a Jeeves to his Wooster—but the truth was that whenever Mister Bob crossed the threshold of Babish's shop, Babish rarely seemed to know who he was.

Babish must, Mister Bob supposed, see a lot of customers in a day. He couldn't be expected to remember them all.

"Ah," said Mister Bob in his customary way, "hello, um, Babish."

Babish had a slightly jaundiced complexion but otherwise resembled the classic London spiv archetype, right down to the pencil moustache. Mister Bob had once overheard a friend of Babish's who had been leaning on Babish's counter in the way another man might prop up a bar and which Mister Bob secretly longed to do, jokingly describe Babish's mustache as "a dirty sanchez" for some reason. Mister Bob supposed this must be the name of the style, though the comment had resulted in laughter he didn't understand. Babish wore the camel-coloured Arkwright-style storekeeper's coat, the well-chewed pencil behind the ear, and the improbably small pork pie hat which, Mister Bob supposed, must have been kept in place through concentrated buttock clenching.

Babish looked confused by Mister Bob's familiar hello but then seemed to recognise him once more.

"Oh yurs," said Babish in a fake posh voice before reverting to the most perfect Cockney accent you've ever heard, "hello guvnor. What can I sort you out with today?"

"I, ah, need, um, soap, Babish," said Mister Bob, flushing.

"Soap is it? Good idea. First row on your left," and Babish nodded in the direction of which he spoke.

Mister Bob turned to find a wire mesh basket filled with individually-wrapped bars of carbolic soap. They looked positively industrial and were probably well-suited to the scouring of years of stench that were draped around Mister Bob's pink body like an ermine cloak.

Even so, Mister Bob had hoped for something lovelier. He quite liked the idea of a nice relaxing soak in the bath upon his return to Portobello and he imagined this would involve something along the lines of the scent of rose petals, a small hardback book perched on the side of the tub, and eucalyptussy vapour lingering in the air.

"Is this, ah, all you have, um, Babish?"

"Well 'ow much more do you need?" asked Babish, "There must be firty bars of soap in there, mate. You planning to wash an elephant or what?"

"Ah," said Mister Bob, "yes, but I was hoping for something, um, well, lovelier."

The word hung in the air. Such a word had probably never been uttered in Babish's shop. The shop was what an academic writer might describe as a "gendered space," mused Mister Bob, who had read widely. It was an overtly male space like an old barbershop, an agricultural store that sold wholesale units of pig swill, or a shack with a sign that read NO GURLS ALLOWED. It reminded him of Mike's Fishing Tackle Shop.

There was a vibrancy to the place that appealed to Mister Bob. He could ignore the poster of Pele, the famous footballer, and enjoy, for example, the mess of bird cages that had been there, unsold, for as long as Mister Bob could remember.

"Ah," said Mister Bob, "that is, it's for my, um, girlfriend."

Something thrilled within Mister Bob at the word "girlfriend." He was not accustomed to using it and doing so had proved a grand adventure. It was then followed by a twinge of guilt because the claim was unauthorised and Tracey was not in reality his girlfriend. Then again, if the only person in the entire world who has given you an iota of affection happens to be female, was it really such slander to describe her as a girlfriend?

"Oh!" said Babish, "girlfriend is it?" and he seemed to Mister Bob to be sizing him up in a new way, squinting slightly as if perhaps only really seeing him for the first time. Paranoid, Mister Bob thought at first that Babish was trying to ascertain whether this girlfriend business was a big sweaty lie, but it was really more like Babish was reassessing Mister Bob's stature as a human being now that a partner existed, somewhere in the world, to vouch for him. "You don't want to be lookin' in 'ere for a present for a young lady, mate. You wanna go dahn Oxford Street or samfin'."

Oxford Street, Mister Bob knew, was practically just around the corner but he did not usually go that far into London on his visits. He usually had a ten- or thirty-minute window of opportunity to catch a train that would get him relatively quickly—if four hours could be described as "relatively quickly" back to Waverley followed by a micron of chit-chat with David McManaman whose head was in the shape of a triangle only he did not seem to know it, and a yellow-windowed bus ride back to his flat. He had, on occasion, gone on London drinking benders, but that had involved staying the night and was usually in Soho or some other literary-and-alcoholic epicentre and nowhere near the commercial citadels of Oxford Street.

"Ah," said Mister Bob, "where would you recommend? On, um, Oxford Street, I mean."

"For soap is it?" said Babish, who took the pencil from behind his ear and used it to scratch the back of his skull and then the inside of his nostril for a thoughtful moment. "You want the Lush shop," he said finally and decisively.

"The, ah, Lush shop," said Mister Bob, "um."

"Yes," said Babish, "the Lush *Spa*, actually. The ladies like to get themselves pampered there. All them Sloane Rangers are at it. But the spa part is upstairs and you don't need to worry about that." There was something in Babish's expression that betrayed he wasn't sure a smelly, moustachioed, 54-year-old man would be welcome at the Lush Spa on Oxford Street though they presumably couldn't turn him away. "Just nip into the shop and they'll have somethin' for ya."

Babish didn't actually give Mister Bob a conspiratorial wink but there was something about his final sentence that implied one.

Babish put the filthy pencil in his mouth jauntily and pawed over some paperwork on a clipboard.

"Thank you, ah, um, Babish," said Mister Bob.

Mister Bob didn't like to leave a shop without buying something, especially when the shop was owned by his excellent good friend Babish.

He browsed the shelves for a while, seeing row upon row of old radios. He looked at a carousel containing adventure paperbacks that must have been there since the 1950s, presumably a time before Babish had even owned the shop. He wondered if the shop had been called Babish back in the day and that the man who stood before him now with a chewed pencil behind his ear was not, in fact, called Babish. Mister Bob didn't really know Babish at all. He wondered, not for the first time, if it was even possible to ever know anyone anyway. In the end, Mister Bob settled on buying a packet of aspirin tablets and a pumice stone.

The pumice stone, Mister Bob reasoned, would be useful in the bath. And there was something appealing about it too. Its rounded but also wedge-like shape reminded him of a clockwork mouse he once had. Where had that clockwork mouse gone? Probably to the same place as Froggo and all the others: quietly discarded without his knowledge. His old friends were never really *his* at all. Ah, well, he had the pumice stone now, for the bath. And, in the meantime, he would enjoy thumbing at it in the trouser pocket of his polyester railway company uniform.

Before he found the courage to venture into the fancy soap shop, Mister Bob went first to a branch of Superdrug near to Euston Station. Mister Bob added a packet of aspirin to his basket, forgetting that he had already bought a packet from Babish.

And then he found his old friend: Mister Matey.

Mister Matey and Mister Bob regarded each other in the bubble bath aisle. Matey was surrounded by other kid-friendly bubble bath bottles in various shapes. There was a Darth Vader one and an impressive robot he knew to be from *Transformers* (though he was surprised that they could still be a going concern after so many years) and various other characters and creatures Mister Bob was not able to identify. He recognised a Winnie-the-Pooh but there was also some sinister-looking thing called an Elsa, which he had never heard of and did not want to know about. But Mister Matey was there, standing and saluting proudly next to his pink partner in nautical crime, Mrs. Matey.

Yes, Mister Matey had a Mrs. Matey. Was it so absurd for Mister Bob to hope for a Mrs. Bob? His pink equivalent must be out there somewhere and he clung to the scant hope that her name was Tracey: Mrs. Tracey Bob.

Mister Bob shook these thoughts from his mind like a dog shaking off pond water and all the associated algae and duck plop. As familiar as it was to him, Mister Bob found Superdug dispiriting and he wanted to get out of there and back to the train station as soon as possible. "All I Want for Christmas is You" was playing on the in-store radio, even though it was barely November. And was it Mister Bob's imagination or was it some sort of lame cover version? No, it must have been real. If Mister Bob's imagination had anything to say about the music being played it would have been something even more terrible.

"Your childhood friends are in the bin /
Mister Bob /
All your friends are in the bin /
Your friends are in the bin /
Mister Bob /
Froggo and Matey and the Duckies too /
And your friends are waiting /
Waiting for you-pooh-pooh, poopy-pee-do..."

There. That was the sort of thing Mister Bob's inadvertently horrible imagination would come up with for just a moment before returning to the saccharine cover version—yes, it really was a cover version sung by some Korean people who didn't seem to understand the lyrics—of "All I want for Christmas is you." What was going on with the world?

He rolled Mister Matey around in the palm of his hand. He was surprised to find the experience unevocative. Few memories returned to him.

There was something different about Mister Matey. He used to be a simple, conical shape, like a skittle, and dark blue in colour. He was now light blue in colour and shaped almost like an hourglass as if symbolising the passage of time, something that was now evidently on Mister Bob's mind.

Matey's face was different to how Mister Bob remembered it too. It was more cartoonish now. And he had *hair*. Mister Matey suddenly had the illusion of tousled blonde hair poking from beneath his hat.

But at least the sailor's hat was still there and you could still unscrew it. That was the nostalgia Mister Bob had been looking for. Advances in computer-aided design, Mister Bob supposed, were responsible for other changes to Matey's appearance, these updated marks of sophistication. Mister Bob wasn't sure if such upgrades were wanted or required or for the better, but the world had moved on and miniature Sailor Men had to keep up.

Sailor Men? Sailor Boys. It occurred to Mister Bob that the people at the company responsible for the production of Mister Matey bath foam had willfully given the mariner a boyish face. It was presumably a move to relate to young people. But whoever heard of a sailor boy? Mister Matey was a *man*, dammit. It would take a grown man to face the ardour of the high seas. His being a little boy all of a sudden made no sense whatsoever.

Mister Bob regarded Mister Matey's new face.

"You've changed," said Mister Bob.

The smell of the soaps, or of natural oils or something, hit him as soon as he crossed the threshold. He'd noticed the smell of Babish's shop and the Superdrug too: the former had smelled sawdusty and turpentiney and the latter had smelled of good value. *This* was something else. The soap shop smelled pink. But also lemony. It was exciting. Mister Bob's senses were inflamed and his eyes became spinning hypno discs.

The place was thronging with young people and nice-looking mums with clear complexions. Mister Bob felt exceptionally out of place. The prices and product descriptions weren't printed on labels like an ordinary shop but written, seemingly dotingly, by hand on miniature blackboards. He didn't know what to make of that. Mister Bob had passed these shops before so their existence was not news to him exactly but he would not have thought to come inside such a place of his own accord. Yesterday it would have felt transgressive, almost as bad as going into a lingerie shop. Now he was inside the lovely soap shop for the first time and it seemed like a magical wonderland.

"Hi!" said a cheerful young woman in an apron, "are you okay there or can I help you with anything?"

"Oh!" said Mister Bob, "ah..."

Mister Bob was going to say that he was "just looking" or that he was indeed "okay there" but, actually, he did need some help and who in the world could possibly help him better than this friendly and forthcoming member of staff? He would ask her for help in treating his stench.

"We have a whole new range of bath bombs and an offer on shower gels over here..." she said.

"...um," said Mister Bob.

"And lotions and..."

"Ah," said Mister Bob, "perhaps, um, you *could* be of some assistance to me."

It may have been Mister Bob's imagination but it seemed to him that the young woman in the apron looked a bit panicked.

"No-no, ah," said Mister Bob needlessly, "it's okay, I would, um, like to buy some nice soap."

The woman brightened. What, wondered Mister Bob, had she thought he was going to do? Toss her over his shoulder and abscond? Out onto a thronging Oxford Street in the middle of the day? Maybe he shouldn't have said "assistance *to me*"? Maybe that was unnecessarily personal? But then Mister Bob remembered his own aversion to speaking to customers in the form of train passengers. It was a form of self-preservation and he could not blame her for it. He suddenly felt more relaxed with this approximation of working-class or service industry kinship in mind. They were not so different, she and he. She was nice-looking while he wore a tie that was too short for him and a pair of very stupid shoes that made him look pompous and off which he had once cleaned vomit in a Glasgow back alley using a greasy Pizza Hut napkin, but they were both service industry professionals and they had both experienced a certain kind of bravery in hiding from customers. He was glad that she could work in a nice apron and not a polyester railway company uniform like his.

"Of course, sir" she said, "what sort of thing did you have in mind?"

"Ah, look," said Mister Bob, "I have no idea. It's just that my, um, girlfriend…"

The shop assistant smiled and visibly relaxed her shoulders when he said "girlfriend." No man with a girlfriend would capture and run away with a shop assistant, he supposed. Tracey was not, of course, in reality, his girlfriend but he allowed himself to think that she was for a delusional moment and it felt nice to say.

"…and, ah, she says, um, I stink."

The shop assistant stopped smiling and tilted her head like a dog would, questioning.

"Reek, actually," confessed Mister Bob, "she said that I reek."

"Oh," said the shop assistant, "hmm. Well, that's okay. Why don't we select three nice kids of soap. They will all smell good in different ways and, after you've used them, you'll know which ones are right for you," she paused, "and which ones your girlfriend likes the most."

Mister Bob blushed.

Together, they went around the shop, selecting soaps from little baskets, Easter morningish. She would hand one to Mister Bob and he would smell it and either accept or reject it. At first, he wasn't sure about ones that smelled musky. He was trying to be less musky. And so he initially leaned towards ones with floral scents and fluttery product names, manliness be damned. He had lived his life up to this point with certain rather conservative and certain rather stupid ideas about masculinity and they had got him nowhere. They had got him into quite a mess, actually, and into a rubbishy pair of shoes he'd once been sick on.

"Come and try these," said the shop assistant.

She took Mister bob over to central bay of metal wash basins. Other people, young women mostly, sniffed at soap bars and tried them out. They gently dried their hands on paper towels and touched their clean hands to their faces to feel the coolness. Some of them applied hand creams, smelling the different types in the free sample pots. How could all of this colour and life exist in the same world as the cardboard bowls of slop people were eating around the corner at Euston? The shop assistant turned on one of the heavy, American-style faucets and water raged forth. She selected a bar soap from a tray of samples and lathered it up in her hands. "Come on," she said.

Cautiously, Mister Bob held out his hands. They were ridiculously pink and he tried not to let them tremble.

She took his hands and pulled him forward with a friendly what-are-you-like-eh? attitude and she applied some of the lather to his hands. She rubbed it onto his fingers a little, which was surprising and a little bit exciting, and then gestured for Mister Bob to continue. He washed his hands with more of the soap.

"What do you think of the aroma?" she asked.

Mister Bob put his wet hands up to his nose and inhaled. It was a musky one.

"Yes, but musky is good," said the shop keeper, "don't you think? And it has complexities. It is earthy. Also, it has glitter. See?"

Mister Bob looked at his hands and turned them over, looking first at the top and then at the palms and then back again. They did in fact glitter. He'd never seen anything like it before. And he liked it. What a good idea.

He noticed the way other people at the sinks were trying and sampling. They had no inhibitions. They just helped themselves. The shop assistants, like shoulder demons in little aprons, encouraged it. He tried to join in. He *did* join in. He was no different to the other customers at the wash basins. He knew the spell would break once he'd left the shop but this was happening now and he wasn't willing to hurry the experience away. The smells and minor ablutions had brought him into a moment, into life, with unusual clarity.

Mister Bob and his shop assistant tried various soaps together. She seemed to have infinite patience. Mister Bob felt grateful and, more than anything, he felt invigorated. There were so many different scents here: orange peel, vanilla, and coconut but also coal-like smells and something like leafmold and ginger and lime and florals and and nutmeg and exotic fruits. And they all combined into an olfactory kaleidoscope.

He tried another. It left a shimmer on his skin. He wondered how it would look on his whole body. Could he report to work with a shimmer? What would Sunny say? What would Tracey think? On balance, Sunny would probably hate it and Tracey would probably like it so this particular bar would be coming home with him without question.

"Should I use any of these on my taint?" asked Mister Bob.

"Um, no, well, it's up to you, I suppose," said the assistant awkwardly.

Mister Bob shrugged it off.

The soaps he eventually settled on were called SNOW FAIRY, LOTUS FLOWER, and GODDESS.

Mister Bob and the shop assistant took the three soaps up to the cash register and she began to ring them through. Mister Bob was happy with his choices and his new prospects as a still-awkward but now stink-free man.

And it was all true. Mister Bob was keen. He greatly looked forward to getting home and to filling the bathtub again and to using his new soaps. In truth, the place had inspired him. Such perfumes! Such ideas! All new to him, yet it had been here all along, nothing special to those in the know. He began to wonder how much of the world had been closed to him only because of his own lack of curiosity or, no that wasn't quite right, his shyness about being alive in the world and away from the book-insulated quietness and genteel squalor of his flat.

"And I'll take one of these too," said Mister Bob, picking up a moisturising cream at random from a countertop display. It wasn't in a tube like his Preparation H but in a darling little pot like a luxury ice cream.

"Certainly," chirped the shop assistant. Clearly, she knew something had shifted in Mister Bob, that something had changed. Her work was done, she knew. Mister Bob suddenly felt shy. This had been his first taste of non-loneliness for quite some time. He'd been admitted, albeit briefly, into the kingdom. Into a Bachelorette Wonderland of softness and care. It was alien, it was gorgeous, and he liked it a lot.

"Thank you," he said.

"And good luck!" she said.

Leaving the shop, Mister Bob plodded to a public bench with only a small amount of seagull crap on it and sat down.

He opened his paper carrier bag and inhaled the mingled scent of his three soaps and single pot of moisturiser in the way a hysteric might try to prevent hyperventilation. He inhaled deeply and a rush of excitement for his bath welled up inside him.

He picked out the moisturiser to see what, precisely, he had bought on a soap-high whim.

It was called LOVELY JUBBLIES.

Mister Bob had one last stop to make with his shopping. He went to a specialist brush shop on Grassmarket in Edinburgh after travelling back on the train. A sign in the window proclaimed that the shop sold all manner of brushes, from brushes to clean the steps of buildings to colourful toothbrushes for children and, most relevantly, "invigorating" scrubbing brushes for bathtime. Grassmarket was on a steep incline and Mister Bob felt notably clammy by the time he reached the shop, which was towards the top of the incline. Still, he was greatly looking forward to putting all of his new toys into action.

He'd noticed the specialist brush shop before, marvelled at how a shop could exist that sold nothing but brushes, and had been curious enough to want to look inside. He'd always put it off though for fear of having to talk with some grizzled old brush expert whose specialist knowledge he would find intimidating. Emboldened by his shopping experiences of the day however, he finally felt ready to go in. He was beginning to understand that there were people in the world who wanted to help.

"Good morrow!" said an energetic young man at the counter. He wore a pair of thick eyeglasses that Mister Bob thought would be unfashionable and a pair of old-fashioned trouser suspenders. He also had a moustache not unlike his own and he wondered if maybe his ridiculous face fungus was back in style after all. Mister Bob wasn't sure what sort of character this young man was. He couldn't read his look at all. He reminded him of the tour guides he sometimes saw escorting crowds of giggling tourists around the Old Town.

"Hello," said Mister Bob, gesturing towards a display of neatly-presented scrubbing brushes, "would any of these do a good job of my taint?"

"Oh no!" said the young man, alarmed, "for that you'll need a much smaller, softer brush. Come right this way, sir."

He escorted Mister Bob to a rack of toothbrush-like brushes. Mister Bob tested the bristled head of one of them with his thumb. It was remarkably soft. Like the down of a baby stoat, he imagined.

"And this will do a bang-up job will it?"

"Girl," said the young man, "you'll be able to eat your dinner off it."

Back in his book-lined flat in Portobello, many hours later, Mister Bob ran another bath. It was the second bath in this noble experiment of eradicating his personal stench. No, what was the word she had used? Reek. Yes, his personal reek.

Perhaps in time Mister Bob would find a way to make his hair grow back thicker and then gain the pride required to no longer be so lonely. Anything, suddenly, seemed possible. But eradicating his reek was the first step. Eradicating his reek was a bridge to betterment, but he was also excited to try his new products. His shopping trip had already changed him.

The water was rumbling into the tub. Though the boiler now was over the initial shock of having to provide hot water on demand and was doing somewhat better this time, the water remained tepid and so Mister Bob resorted to boiling kettles once again. Perhaps three or four kettles this time would suffice instead of six.

But now it was fun time. Mister Bob could unleash the bubbles. He twisted off the sailor hat cap from Mister Matey's head and emptied his green flowing brains into the bathwater. It frothed immediately and gloriously into a fluffy white foam just as Mister Bob had remembered it from when he was a boy.

Mister Bob then unwrapped one of his lovely new soaps. After some deliberation he chose the one called GODDESS. Wrapper off, it was black. Like a block of coal. It had a commanding, obelisk-like presence and a rich, complex, spicy, somehow ancient aroma. It looked like a dark stone and the longer he admired it and rolled it around in the palm of his hand, the more he appreciated that it wasn't just black but that it had complex colour tones and patterns. It also had gold glitter in it.

The water continued to run and to rumble while the bubble bath continued to foam. His old bar of soap, the simple white one, looked stupid next to the new ones.

Curiosity got the better of Mister Bob and he hurriedly opened the other two bars of soap. As he suspected, each one was its own mysterious colour and had its own special smell. SNOW FAIRY wasn't as complex as the GODDESS bar but was little-girly and playful. He'd originally meant to keep two bars of soap wrapped and stored in the little bathroom drawer for future bathtime excursions, but now he saw that the only way to go about this was to try all three and to *use* all three each time he had a bath. Not only would it bust his stink, which he had covertly analysed on the five-hour train journey back from London and decided was reminiscent of root vegetables, but it would leave him smelling complexly botanical. People would want to follow him around. People who knew the word would call him a "popinjay." Mister Bob realised he would be perfectly happy to be called a popinjay. Root vegetables had their place in the world, Mister Bob decided, but no human being should smell like root vegetables, especially so consistently or earthily.

Mister Bob went to the kitchen to collect the last boiled kettle. He took it back to the bathroom, kicking his way through more junk mail and Farmfoods circulars that had piled up during his absence, and poured the water gently into the tub. It made him feel like an Hellenic eunuch, pouring water so luxuriously into a bath. The real eunuchs probably didn't pour from a kettle labelled RUSSELL HOBBS though. On the other hand, they wouldn't have had the companionship of Mister Matey either.

Mister Bob tested the water with his elbow.

The bath was ready.

Lowering himself into the bath, the skin of his back made a familiar *squoinkle* noise against the side of the tub. The rubbery folds of his fat, not normally rubbery-feeling in regular life but somehow changed in the world of the bathtub, rumbled like michelin tyres down the side of the tub as he sank down and allowed the water to cover his shoulders.

The Matey bubble bath smelled good, refreshing, and it filled his nostrils. It seemed to go *through* his nostrils like the appetising smell of a pie in an old cartoon. Some of the foam became trapped between his shoulders and the bathtub, a crinkly sensation he had not felt for a long time, and it tickled the bottom of his hairline at the nape of his neck. A memory came back to Mister Bob that you shouldn't allow the Matey bubble bath to get into your hair lest it cause dandruff.

The information about dandruff, trivial though it was, had been lost to Mister Bob for all this time. Being submerged in warm water changed his state of mind so utterly, connected him so viscerally with his past, that a memory from at least forty years ago had come to the surface. It struck him as truly remarkable.

And then Mister Bob remembered another thing about bathtime.

Throwing dandruff caution to the wind, Mister Bob lowered himself further so that his ears were submerged and only his face and forehead, framed by bath foam, and his bent knees and his paunch remained above the water. His view was of the ceiling now, soft artex not of his choosing, and the sounds of the room had become muffled.

Mister Bob listened.

It was quiet for a moment but then he could hear him.

"Mumfle-mumfle, brilla-breckin-baa," said Pavel.

Or he said something along those lines anyway. Mister Bob could hear the measured rumble of conversation from the downstairs room. He hadn't thought of that for decades and he'd completely forgotten about the effect. The sounds of Pavel talking were travelling up the old building's pipework between Pavel's living room and Mister Bob's bathroom.

Mister Bob stifled a laugh.

"Mahahaha!" said someone else, "meh-haha-ha-haaa!"

A woman's laughter! It was a lovely, lilting feminine laugh. There could be no mistaking it. Pavel had a girlfriend and she was visiting his flat. And they were having *fun*.

Mister Bob was filled with a sickening envy and he rose up out of the water, enraged.

It had sounded to Mister Bob like Pavel—Pavel!—was really holding court down there. It sounded like Pavel's companion was genuinely enjoying his stories. What did Pavel—Pavel!—have to say that could be so amusing? What about trains could possibly interest a humourful young woman?

Mister Bob sighed and reached for the GODDESS

soap. He rolled it in his hands and admired its mysterious blackness. He snorked some of its musky, dark-floral vapour. As it filled his head, Mister Bob re-found his composure. He was suddenly surprised that he could feel envy towards Pavel and his girlfriend. This was new to Mister Bob and, through the sickly pea soup of envy, it interested him.

Miser Bob lathered his armpits with foam from the GODDESS bar. The foam was white, which he had not expected. Bathtime was full of surprises for Mister Bob. It was so far turning out to be a time of genuine discovery.

He lathered the back of his neck, making sure to get into the creases surrounding the fold of bristly fat behind his skull which he'd once mistakenly thought might contain his cerebellum, distended from so much reading.

He lathered the front and sides of his neck, his shoulders, his chest, his... yes, his breasts, and he remembered another bathtime observation from childhood, that the soap in the water would make the bubbles go flat.

He didn't want to make the bubbles go flat yet. As much as anything, the foam bubbles obscured his penis whose fishing float-like drifting he had, last time, found faintly depressing.

Mister Bob submerged himself again, letting the warmish water cover his shoulders, and he closed his eyes. He smelled the smells: the chemical sting of Mister Matey, the psychotic hopscotch of SNOW FAIRY, the eternal unknowability of GODDESS, how they intermingled. He opened them again and swivelled his eyeballs around without moving his head or craning his neck, and he took in some of the sights of the bathroom: it was all quotidian, perfectly familiar, to him but at the same time Mister Bob found that he'd never really looked at any of it before.

He swiped that thought from his mind. Mister Bob was not ready for a phenomenological review of the bathroom. He would leave such things for the writers of the books he liked to read on the train. Simone de Beauvoir. Karl Jaspers. His personal favourite was Georges Perec.

Bathtime struck him now as profligate. Wonderfully, bubblingly profligate. The shower, the aggressively named "power shower," had come to dominate Western washing.

But then he pushed that thought from his mind too. Mister Bob did not want to intellectualise this.

He washed the lather from his body and lathered his face. Another memory surfaced about covering his entire body with soap lather and surprising his mother by saying "look, Mummy, I'm a *white* man!" to which she had said, "yes dear." That was always her placating way of ending a conversation when she was tired. Yes dear.

Mister Bob reflected that his mother was often tired, had been tired for as long as he knew her and all the way to the end. It can't have been easy to have been a suburban mum with no money in the 1970s. Mister Bob had always known this but he only really understood and accepted it now somehow, as he sat in the bathtub, his second proper bath in at least as many decades.

The bathwater was once again tepid. It hadn't been satisfactorily hot to begin with and Mister Bob vowed again to find out what was wrong with the boiler and to get it fixed.

Mister Bob wondered if he would really do this. He had vowed many times to remove the ocean of junk mail from the entry hall floor but he had not yet found the strength. No, not the strength exactly. Or even the time. It was *bandwidth* he lacked. *Capacity*. If Mister Bob could not find the bandwidth or the capacity to accomplish even that much, what chance had he got with the rest of his masterplan?

Things were getting maudlin. Tepid bathwater will do that to you and it did it effortlessly with Mister Bob who, he reflected, was weak to begin with.

Mister Bob washed the soap lather from his face. He didn't mind if the Mister Matey bubble bath foam went flat now. He was almost ready to end his second bath.

He took a hold of the SNOW FAIRY soap, this one a more orthodox pink, and used it to lather his legs and feet and around the sides of his genitals.

He lathered his genitals.

He lathered his penis and the peculiar little crab's eye stalk that sprouted from the tip of his foreskin.

He stretched around and lathered his buttocks, taking care to lather his arsecrack as instructed, which Mister Bob now realised must serve as a trough for capturing and storing human body odour.

A slight pain, a sting, issued from his anus and Mister Bob realised that the water or possibly the SNOW FAIRY had aggravated his haemorrhoids.

As well as gingivitis and athlete's foot, another of Mister Bob's personal problems was haemorrhoids. He parted the Mister Matey bubble bath foam with the backs of his hands so that he could look through the water. He was curious to know if his haemorrhoids were bleeding. He expected to see a skein of blood rising in the water like smoke from an extinguished candle.

Mister Bob was disappointed. He did not see a skein of blood rising in the water like smoke from an extinguished candle because the bathwater had become cloudy with two kinds of soap.

He used one of the scrubbing brushes he'd bought in Edinburgh, taking care not to scrub too hard and damage his skin. He applied some of the GODDESS sop to the tips of the bristles and scrubbed his armpits again. It felt good. It felt *cleansing*, which was, of course, the entire point. But psychologically cleansing as well as something merely on the surface of the skin.

State memory. Pile pain. Nice soaps. Scrub. It had been an eventful bathtime for Mister Bob.

He wanted more things next time. Not just lovely soap and Mister Matey, though they had all been wonderful to experience, but he wanted hotter water. He wanted music. And he wanted the BATH BOMBS and all the rest of it. He'd return to that shop and speak to the apron-wearing shop assistant once again and this time he would take a large carrier bag with him. He knew there was one under the sink in the kitchen. It was orange-coloured and had come from Sainsbury's but he was embarrassed to use it because it had a picture of an elephant on it and the word "JUMBO."

Mister Bob pulled the bath plug and sat in the water as the tub emptied. It gave the illusion that he was rising out of the water like one of those islands that briefly emerge from the ocean once every twelve or eighteen years before returning again to mysterious depths.

Mister Bob emptied his head of thought as the water went down. Like many other people, he had idly wondered before if it was possible to truly think of nothing, but on this occasion Mister Bob really did empty his head. He thought of nothing whatever for several seconds. His mind was gradually, he hoped, finding some sort of peace.

Mister Bob wondered if sitting in the bathtub as it slowly emptied was the only circumstance in which a person could successfully think of nothing whatever. He reflected that, in this case, it was because he was relaxed for the first time in a long time. Despite some melancholy feelings prompted by the reactivation of some old memories and despite that sense of poisonous envy he had briefly felt when hearing the giddy lilting laugh of Pavel's girlfriend as he unfairly eavesdropped through his own bathwater, Mister Bob felt *relaxed*. Mister Bob felt *refreshed*. Mister Bob had not experienced a single one of his waking nightmares, his "visions," either. He had completely forgotten about his fear of falling through the floor.

The last of the water gurgled away, taking with it some but not all of the humanish dregs of bathtime soup.

The exit pipe of the bathtub seemed to inhale the last of the water.

Mister Bob sat in the otherwise empty tub, wet and clammy. He stood slowly, pushing up with his arms against the sides of the tub, and then threw his first leg out of the tub onto the shaggy safety of the bathmat.

As his foot touched down on dry terrain, he exchanged a glance with Mister Matey and said "land ho!" though he didn't expect a little boy like this new incarnation of Matey to appreciate nautical jargon.

Mister Bob thought briefly—as he had done about the RUSSELL HOBBS kettle earlier, remembering how he had stood in line at Argos shortly after moving into his rented Portobello flat—about his acquisition of that bathmat. He couldn't remember where it had come from. It probably came with the flat and, as such, had been there for fifteen, no sixteen, years, and probably longer.

As he considered the fungal universe the bathmat most certainly harboured, Mister Bob vowed to get a new one. There was something sinister about that bathmat anyway. It looked like it might start crawling around erratically.

Standing on the bath mat while furthering the life of its fungal and probably *Horton Hears a Who!*-esque inhabitants by slowly dripping into it, Mister Bob reached for his towel, which hung on a peg, to dry off.

The towel was old and frayed. It was torn slightly at the hemline. Mister Bob vowed to buy another towel at the same time as another bath mat. He almost didn't want to. He saw the towel practically as an old friend, that there was life in the old dog yet, and that it would be treacherous of him to replace it.

And yet this whole thing, this noble experiment in taking baths, was about accessible indulgence and luxury, he now knew. So why not? He deserved a soft, fluffy towel and not a once-proud, now-tattered rag like something you'd see hanging from a lamppost in a Belfast suburb.

On making this decision, much as when he had bought the various soaps in Lush, Mister Bob felt suddenly dignified in a way he had not in a long time. Potentially, he mused, he had never felt such dignity, so these increments in dignity-raising were significant.

Mister Bob was on the right path for the first time since childhood and he was enjoying it. He didn't need to work out or understand the mistakes of the past. He could just start again. 53, sorry, 54 wasn't old. He could live just as long again, properly this time, starting right now. Starting, in fact, last week when he'd drawn that first bath. His stink was all but gone. He was glistening. His skin had sparkle.

Mister Bob raised his towel-grasping hand above his head and gingerly sniffed his armpit. The armpit, Mister Bob was mildly nonplussed to note, smelled like neither a goddess nor a snow fairy. Not that he knew precisely what either of those types should smell like. But at least the armpit conveyed absolutely no stench of root vegetables. Or did it? Maybe, despite everything, there was still an ever-so-faint whiff.

Maybe these things had to be achieved in stages. Today, in a diary-worthy event, he had all but eradicated his root vegetable reek. If anything was left of it, hardly a soul would notice. Tomorrow perhaps he would achieve that goddess or snow fairy smell.

Mister Bob dried his hair. He used a patting motion rather than the rubbing motion to which he was naturally inclined. He was concerned about his thinning hair and now imagined that a gentle patting motion when drying his hair would help to retain what was left of it. Nobody had told him to do this. It was his own theory.

Mister Bob dried his arms and legs, deciding to continue the patting motion on his skin so as to absorb moisture into the towel but not damage his skin with the towel's elderly coarseness. All of this would later strike Mister Bob as mildly curious. He had never taken such delicate care of his body before. He was far more accustomed to treating it roughly just to get through the day, to throwing his hips as he walked, to charging breathlessly along train platforms and up tenement steps in vain attempts to look strong or not exhausted, a confidence trick to convince *himself* that he was strong and not exhausted. He had not felt so inclined to be delicate with his body until this, his second bath. He knew now that he needed to take care of his body. If he wanted it to last another 54 years, so that he was not shortchanged any further by life, he would need to be delicate with it. Starting now.

If these baths were to be a Great Experiment, he reasoned that perhaps he should record the results. After drying off, Mister Bob decided, he would write some notes in one of the many unused notebooks he'd acquired over the years. "Bath 1," he would write, "slight nightmare, multiple visions, temporary suspension of ah and um." And "Bath 2," he would write, resulted in "near-complete eradication of stench."

Mister Bob dried his tummy. Yes, it was big but it was also somehow firm, which made him glad. He was firm like a Space Hopper or one of those gymnastic balls he'd seen in the windows of suburban houses and sometimes the backyards as he'd blasted past them on trains. Maybe this was something Tracey liked about him. His firmness. And he did not stink, did not "reek," anymore.

Mister Bob dab-dried his face and neck and collar bone and breasts and buttocks and haunches and then his face again. He used the tattered old towel like floss to dry his back. It did not feel wholly effective, Mister Bob mused, and perhaps a new towel was really a necessity as well as a luxury.

Mister Bob felt invigorated after his bath. Mister Bob felt virile. Mister Bob was all man. But in a new way. He was shimmering, bubble-gum-scented and virile.

He mused that might be some sort of bathtime "aftercare" he could indulge in. Something to seal the deal after his scrub in the tub and after drying off.

There was, of course.

He rifled through the paper carrier bag, which he'd placed atop of the toilet lid, and produced a small plastic pot.

LOVELY JUBBLIES, said the pot, BREAST CREAM. And then, "LADIES, IT'S TIME TO TAKE CARE OF YOUR PAIR."

There came a Sunny-esque banging at the door.

How odd, thought Mister Bob and wrapped the towel around his waist. He assumed that perhaps it was Pavel since it was Pavel who had last knocked, during his previous bath.

Mister Bob was still naked from the waist up. His nipples were pink like the snouts of moles. Were they *too* pink? Mister Bob found them somehow vulgar. But how could a natural human body be vulgar? He couldn't help how he looked to that extent. He had been taught by culture to be ashamed of his body and this shame extended to his pink nipples. They weren't too pink. There was no such thing. They were what they were.

Even so, he made a mental note to keep his shirt on if he ever became naked with Tracey or anybody else.

Mister Bob made his way to the door, kicking again through the litter of Farmfoods circulars and Domino's Pizza menus. He wondered briefly whatever had happened to Pizza Hut. Didn't they used to reign supreme? Pizza Hut—Hit the Hut!—had been gross to begin with but Domino's had come along at some point in the meantime with an even steeper descent into gastronomic Hell.

Perhaps it would not be Pavel at the door at all but some kind of delivery van driver, but he could not guess what they would be delivering since he was not one for ordering anything other than books, which came in the regular post. Or perhaps a charity collector someone had annoyingly let into the building. A glimpse of his nipples, Mister Bob reasoned, would see them off. They would understand immediately that they were invading his privacy and be off.

Mister Bob opened the door.

It was, unfortunately, Mrs. Cuntapples.

Mrs. Cuntapples looked, as she always did, as if she were sucking a super-sour gobstopper. The drag lines from a younger life spent sucking at cigarettes had done this to her. It gave the impression that her lips were perpetually pursed with rage.

"*Mister* Forrester," said Mrs. Cuntapples, "I can hear you splashing around in there, you know. And the sound of pipes and floorboards protesting in dismay. It is all most unusual. I hope you are not squandering the hot water for the rest of us in this building."

"Oh," said Mister Bob, "Ah, I'm, um, very sorry Mrs. Buntapples."

"*Sorry*, Mister Forrester," said Mrs. Cuntapples, "will not cut the mustard. How am I supposed to wash my little Bistro without a basic amenity like hot water because some ungainly... *sybarite* has squandered it all by luxuriating for hours on end in a *bath*?"

"I beg your pardon, Mrs. Buntapples," said Mister Bob, "but wash your little *what*?"

"My little Bistro, Mister Forrester, *Bistro*. My miniature pinscher."

When this evidently meant nothing additional to Mister Bob, Mrs. Buntapples was moved to clarify, "My wee *dug*."

"Oh," said Mister Bob, still a little bewildered by the intrusion, much less Mrs. Cunapples' lack of interest in his drippiness or his nipples or the shabby condition of the towel now wrapped around his waist. A less psychotic personality would have noticed the busyness of the person whose bathtime they had interrupted, or perhaps sensed their general vulnerability while unclothed. But not the rancid Mrs. Cuntapples. The words "wee dug," however, exposed her true accent slightly, which Mister Bob found momentarily charming.

"Your little..."

"*Bistro*," said Mrs. Cuntapples furiously.

"Bistro," said Mister Bob, "is a very lovely ah,

doggie, but, um, he's hardly my responsibility, is he now?"

Mrs. Cuntapples' face went purple. She was not used to being challenged or even questioned, especially by a tenant. She looked as if the top of her head was about to flip open like a pedal bin and possibly molten lava would run down her furious face.

"Not your responsibility?!"

"No, Mrs. Buntapples. With all due respect, your dog isn't my responsibility. All I did was have a bath. I do, after all, ah, pay my, um, rent."

"Pay your *rent*?" said Mrs. Cuntapples. She hissed the word "rent" like a Gorgon, but her rage seemed to have deescalated marginally, perhaps because she was on more familiar landlordly territory now. "And on time, I suppose?"

"Yes, Mrs. Buntapples, I always pay on time."

"Hah!" said Mrs. Cuntapples, inexplicably.

"Have I ever failed to pay my rent to you on time, Mrs. Buntapples?"

Mrs. Cuntapples pursed her lips until they looked like a gouged eye. But no answer was forthcoming.

"Mrs. Buntapples..." said Mister Bob, not noticing that his old companions, "ah" and "um," had fled but dimly aware that he was more emboldened than he normally would be in confrontational circumstances. She had come into *his* world, after all, his new world of bubble baths and GODDESS soaps, and not he into hers. Even so, he had not previously imagined ever being able to take a stand, even a small stand, against

Mrs. Cuntapples. "...I asked you a question. Have I ever failed to pay my rent on time?"

"I would have to check my records," said Mrs. Cuntapples primly, "And I do keep records, Mister Forrester, *most copious and sophisticated records!*"

"I am not interested in your record keeping, Mrs. Buntapples," said Mister Bob, clutching his raggedy towel, "much as I am not interested in your dog or when he gets his bathtime. I pay my rent like everyone else in this building and part of what we pay for is the freedom to bathe, to cleanse our hard-working bodies, whenever we please."

Mister Bob congratulated himself internally for saying "bathe" and not "take a fucking bath," which would have risked another potential peddle bin head lid flip. He was also glad not to have said anything about being "within his rights," which would have made him a trespasser in her territory of tenants' rights and rent books. An old-fashioned/ landlady like Mrs. Cuntapples would have a series of stock responses for tenants claiming to be "within their rights," so he'd steered clear of the phrase entirely.

"And what's more, Mrs. Buntapples," said Mister Bob, "I don't think I'm capable of using up all of the hot water. I don't think that's how hot water works. The building, so far as I know, does not have a limited supply. I have what is known as a combination boiler, which heats the water for this flat and this flat alone."

He had looked it up in a book. Knowledge is power and today Mister Bob wielded it like a broadsword.

"*You* have a combination boiler do you?!" snapped Mrs. Cuntapples, "You have a combination boiler?!"

The landlord class, and Mister Bob had observed this before, never miss an opportunity to remind their tenants that their homes are not their own.

"I rent one," said Mister Bob firmly, before adding, "as you well know."

"*Well*," said Mrs. Cuntapples in an offended tone but one that betrayed her awareness of there being no tuft of wild grass on the moral high ground left for her to cling to, "of all the..."

"Of all the what, Mrs. Buntapples," said Mister Bob, "of all the what? Of all the *nerve* perhaps? The *nerve* for paying my rent on time every single month and finally finding the gumption to use the bathtub and the boiler I've been paying for all these years? The *nerve* for objecting to your latest crude little campaign to make your tenants feel small? The *nerve* for living my life as I intend, from this day on, to live it?"

"Ah," said Mrs. Cuntapples, "um."

"And since we're on the subject of the combination boiler that I *rent* from you, it doesn't work properly. As it is your property and not mine, as you so correctly point out, I expect you will be certain to send someone to repair it at the earliest opportunity. BECAUSE MY BATHWATER IS TEPID!"

Mister Bob slammed the door.

Mister Bob released his grip on the towel and it fell to the floor making a papery sound among the Farmfoods circulars and the Domino's Pizza menus.

Mister Bob savoured the feeling of the air circulating around his bits.

Mister Bob was very proud of himself.

He hadn't even said Cuntapples.

Four

Mister Bob stood in his kitchen and stared at the RUSSELL HOBBS kettle. It rattled slightly and a coil of steam unwound from the spout as it edged closer to boiling point.

Mister Bob stared at the kettle until his eyes blurred.

In the bathroom, the water rumbled gaily from the unsupervised bath tap, its sound mildly muffled by a fluffy landscape of Matey bubbles.

Mister Bob thought about what would happen if the kettle suddenly exploded and lashed him with hot water. Was the water yet hot enough to scald him? He wasn't certain but he assumed the worst. The kettle would explode, Mister Bob decided, and poach his face like an egg. It would explode, the kettle would, and destroy his face and he would spend the rest of his days trying to go about his business while looking like somebody from a cautionary public information film for the children of the 1970s. His mutilated complexion would be yet another thing for him to be shy about in life on top of everything else. Mister Bob would be a bachelor with gingivitis and haemorrhoids and thinning hair and a melted face and the words "the... the... the kettle just, ah-um, exploded" forever on his lips.

Not content with this idea, perhaps curious as to why this idle fantasy wasn't one of his involuntary and fully immersive Panic Visions, which was the name he now had for them, Mister Bob tried to explode the kettle with his mind. Insanely, he tried to explode the kettle with the psychic powers he did not believe he had. A couple of mind bullets would take care of that kettle and his fate along with it.

Mister Bob sometimes did this. He might notice a passenger jet or a helicopter overhead and he'd fire mind bullets at it in an attempt to shoot it down. It didn't mean anything because he knew he had no magic powers. And at the same time, Mister Bob knew that if an aircraft were to fall from the sky after he'd fired his mind bullets, it would be enough of a shock to put him in a mental asylum for the rest of his days.

Mister Bob was not sure why he did this.

The kettle popped, making Mister Bob jump. He wondered for a moment if this hadn't been one of his Panic Visions after all, a particularly sophisticated one that had given the illusion of his staring at the kettle and thinking about how this wasn't a Vision when, in fact, it was one.

Mister Bob put the thought out of his head. He really had no idea about it anyway.

Mister Bob had a bath to fill. He took the boiled kettle into the bathroom and added its steaming contents to the foaming water.

Putting the kettle down on the closed toilet lid, he checked the water temperature in the bathtub with his elbow in what had become his customary way—three instances, reasoned Mister Bob, was the minimum number for an event to become customary—and knew that he was ready for his third soak in the tub.

He took pause to notice that he was looking forward to getting into the water this time, that the anxiety and floor-collapsing fantasies of his earlier forays into bathtime had long fled.

Mister Bob unbuttoned his shirt.

Mister Bob looked at his reflection in the mirror and stroked his moustache with his hand. There were two mirrors in Mister Bob's bathroom, a medium-sized wall-mounted mirror and a small circular shaving mirror that craned out over the wash basin on a concertina arm. For a moment, Mister Bob's moustache was visible to him in both mirrors.

Mister Bob wondered if he should shave his moustache off today. It was one of the things, like the too-short necktie and the overly formal shoes, that made him look pitiable. A moustache had suited the young fellow in the brush shop but Mister Bob didn't know what it all meant. That brush shop fellow had been in some sort of club Mister Bob wasn't a member of. The non-affiliated moustache clinging to his old-man face looked decidedly rubbishy. If some rough kids on bikes saw him in the street, they might shout "oi, moustache," before speeding away, laughing. This had never happened to Mister Bob. It was only an idea, like the kettle exploding. It had often struck him, however, that the moustache *might* be one of the things that made people think twice about sitting next to him on the bus or prompt a jester to goose him when the Festival was on.

On the other hand, his moustache was not anything Tracey had complained about when she'd candidly and drunkenly lambasted him for his stink (*the word was "reek,"* he kept reminding himself) on that special birthday night on the sleeper train. Mister Bob was close to certain that she would have mentioned it at the same time if she disliked his moustache. For all Mister Bob knew, Tracey was tremendously sexually aroused by his moustache.

Mister Bob decided not to shave his moustache off this time and he admired it again in the twin mirrors. He *frisked* it. He blurred his eyes and tried to relate it to the younger man's moustache in the brush shop. The two moustaches weren't so far removed. He and the brush shop guy were brothers in face fuzz.

Before getting in the tub, which was lightly steaming from five kettles of boiled water but still barely smogging up the room, Mister Bob took in the rest of his body as it was reflected in the larger of the two mirrors. He let out a sigh and then watched as his cheeks flapped.

His paunch hung slightly over the indentation made by his belt buckle but the paunch was firm and almost like a pregnancy bulge. It didn't swing or wobble when he moved from side to side. Maybe Tracey would walk up to him one day and place her cool palms on the sides of his paunch, just to feel its warmth.

He had no idea.

Since he'd been bathing with his new soaps, his skin had begin to glimmer. It gave his naked body a slightly magical aura. It was either the golden glitter from the GODDESS soap or else the effect of taking better care of oneself, some inner improvement shining though. Whether from glitter or some internal resource that comes with a well-scrubbed soul, his belly gleamed.

Why did he have a big belly? He didn't eat a great deal more than anyone else. In fact he often skipped meals if his work schedule made it difficult to get lunch or find the time for breakfast before an early train. The booze didn't help, of course. His was probably a beer belly. Or maybe it was the Farmfoods crap or the Domino's pizza he ate when he didn't have the strength, no, the *bandwidth*, to prepare real food when he came home from London or Inverness or Aberdeen in the middle of the night. It was booze, a bad diet, and anxiety of course. He also had to cramp his movements all the time in the confined spaces on the trains; he spent a lot of time on his feet but none of it was exercise since it led to little energetic motion. Or did anxiety actually help in weight *loss*? All the nervous jittering? He put the issue of weight to one side and continued the guided tour of his body.

Mister Bob explored his belly button in an act of literal navel gazing. He gently pulled it apart with his fingertips, never having really considered his bellybutton as an aperture before, and saw a tuft of blue-coloured belly button fluff inside. The blue colour was the same colour as his polyester railway company shirt, presumably a collection of gradually accumulated polyester fibres. He pulled it out with pincer fingers and was surprised to find that it was wet, presumably with his own sweat, and almost oily. Where he'd pulled it out, the area felt newly cold as the fresh air rushed in. He balled the tuft up like a bogey and then flicked it into the water of the toilet bowl where it made a satisfying *ploop!* sound.

Returning to the belly button, Mister Bob splayed it open a little further and examined it even more closely. There was a sort of off-brown earwaxy residue in there. He plucked an ancient cotton bud from a dusty container of its fellows and, on moistening it between his lips, polished the brown residue away. Part of it had solidified into a grit-like substance in a particularly difficult crevice and Mister Bob felt the air caress the tiny cavity upon prising it out with the tip of the bud. It felt uniquely satisfying to have prised out such a tiny piece of grit, a miniscule *Excalibur*. There was something almost sacred about a belly button. A bellybutton, Mister Bob mused, was an origin story, a personal Bolt's Farm or Bethlehem stable. To look into it was like looking into the distant past, almost like how the stars of the night sky are million-year-old points of light. For this reason, he decided, it was good to keep it clean and he would do so from now on.

It was harder to imagine anyone being interested in his penis and testicles. Unlike his paunch, they did at least swing when he moved from side to side. Most of the motion was in the penis, small as it was. His balls, being larger and heavier, lagged behind ever-so-slightly in their pendulum motion. The crab's eye-like growth on Mister Bob's foreskin looked drowsy today, half asleep.

His public hair—had he *once* looked at or thought about it since adolescence?—was an excitement of messy and greying scrub. Never had it crossed his mind to try and improve it in any way. "Manscaping," they called the art of trimming a man's pubic hair to make it more aesthetically appealing. Mister Bob had learned the word when he'd read something about it in a tabloid newspaper over someone's shoulder on a train. Like the moustache, he decided against tampering with it today. He had, after all, absolutely no idea what he was supposed to do. Did one trim it with scissors? And, if so, should he use the little scissors with which he sometimes clipped his toenails or should he use the big ones from the kitchen that he used for trimming bacon fat? Or were you supposed to pluck them out one by one? Or was some other device, possibly involving hot wax, supposed to be involved? How did other people know what to do about this? Did they talk about it? Why was he so out of the public loop? Mister Bob had no idea and did not want to think about trimming or plucking or waxing his pubic hair for popular appeal. It struck him as absurd.

His breasts hung a little low and he felt a needle of self-consciousness again about his overly-pink nipples. There was a little bit of hair around them too, but it was a gingery blond colour and nothing like the colour of his public hair or the hair on his head or in his moustache at all. It was amazing how the human body— or at least the body of Mister Bob—could produce such a bewildering diversity of fuzz.

Mister Bob's legs were short but actually quite strong. They were probably strong from all the time he spent walking up and down train aisles and dashing along platforms to make connections.

Mister Bob's nose was bigger than what people probably thought of as ideal and it looked like a sweet potato.

There was a patch of eczema languishing beneath Mister Bob's left armpit. It was an all-too familiar patch of eczema, seemingly always there. Much like the crab's eye that was growing down below and would one day become a tendril, the eczema patch was an almost reliable sight. A zany thought crossed Mister Bob's mind involving his body as a landscape. If miniature people, gnomes or something, should be walking around and living their lives on his skin, this eczema patch would be a landmark to them. They could navigate by it or use it as a reliable meeting place. To the body gnomes, it wouldn't be an eczema match but the eczema patch, as in, "turn north-north-west at the eczema patch."

Mister Bob's feet were flat, and some little black hairs sprouted from the largest toes. His toes, like his fingers, were stumpy. He had never really looked at them before, not with a critical eye at any rate. They looked terrible to him though, like grey little pearls.

Just as Mister Bob was trying to find the courage to turn around and look at himself from behind, a sharp, cold draft came from under the bathroom door. It trickled over his feet and spiralled partway up his leg before he decided that now was probably the time to get into his bath.

Finally, Mister Bob relaxed in his bath. Thanks to the fine art of topping up the tub with kettles of boiling water, pacing back and forth between kitchen and bathroom with his fantasy explosives, it was plenty warm enough.

Mister Bob sighed a sigh of relief as he felt his body temperature slowly but definitely rise. The temperature rise began with the heating of the cool and camelish fat deposits close to the surface of his skin, around his belly and buttocks and thighs, and continued until it reached his core.

Mister Bob mused that if there were any body gnomes journeying upon him at this moment, they should muster back to whichever crevice they preferred to hide in when their world became submerged. Was every submergence in bathwater an apocalypse to the body gnomes? A major geological event like an Ice Age? Would tomorrow's body gnome historians say things like "not so very long ago, this vast terrain was under water." It was funny to Mister Bob how vividly he could see them in his mind's eye. He should write a disgusting kids' book.

Mister Bob's actual eyes saw a different story: the story that he should clean the tiles before his next bath. If this was all about luxury, about personal indulgence and reclaiming his dignity, Mister Bob could do better in terms of his surroundings. He realised that he had meant to arrange music. It would be easy and would merely involve downloading an app to his phone, but he'd forgotten to do it because he disliked fiddling with technology. Cleaning the tiles, reducing the neon pink fungal sheen from the grout, would make these bathing experiences feel marginally closer to, say, being at the Real Alcázar of Seville than, say, the set of the TV comedy series *Bottom*. In his newly relaxed state, Mister Bob felt that anything was possible but he also knew how many times he'd vowed, and then failed, to reclaim his entry hall from the Farmfoods circulars and the Domino's Pizza menus.

Mister Bob submerged himself until his whole head was momentarily underwater. A notion crossed the news desk inside his mind that he could kill himself this way, accidentally or by design, but he dismissed it.

He effortlessly dismissed the idea as one might swipe away a strand of spider's silk.

Before he surfaced, Mister Bob got the impressions of conversation downstairs in Pavel's flat. He wasn't interested in whether they were the voices of girlfriends this time; instead it made him think of childhood again. More memories came to him of that bathroom in the past and he wondered if this telephone system between bathrooms of past and present would ever be of a high enough resolution for him to leave even the bathroom of the past and to feel his way around in the world of 1968. How far could he get? Would he be captured and returned to his bath as a naked five-year-old covered in soap (*"Look Mummy, I'm a white man!"*) or would he be allowed to drift freely around in the past like a visiting ghost?

Mister Bob remembered his mother clipping his fingernails over the toilet bowl, telling him to keep still, to stop fidgeting, and that it would all be over and done with in a moment.

Mister Bob remembered putting a bare and still-damp foot up to the avocado-green rim of the 1968 toilet bowl and dusting his young feet with something called Tinaderm Powder. Tinaderm Powder! Of course! *That* was why athlete's foot had gone extinct!

Mister Bob remembered that the sound he would most commonly hear when submerged beneath his childhood bathwater was the sound of pompous hymn singing on *Songs of Praise* on the television. Was Sunday the only day on which young Mister Bob—Master Bob—

had a bath? He rather thought it was. Still, once a week was better than never, which had been Mister Bob's routine after a certain point in his life. He wondered now how he'd fallen into a state of such terrible entropy. What must people have thought of him? This unclean stinker? He was lucky anyone gave him the time of day at all. He was lucky to have a job, to know Tracey and Sunny and Babish and Pavel, and for them all to occasionally talk to him. He'd been entombed, socially insulated, by years of stink.

Mister Bob remembered *bath pearls*. How was that for an archaic 1970s consumer product? Bath pearls. He'd never quite known what they were but he supposed now that they were water-soluble balls containing pleasant-smelling oils. When he'd been small, he'd wanted to eat them because they'd looked so tasty. This had been his response when he'd first opened the GODDESS soap at the age of 54, so he hadn't changed much.

As Mister Bob surfaced, face and head oily with bath foam, he was struck again by the vividness of the pink fungus in the tile grouting. He really *must* clean the tiles before his next bath. It was pinker even than his nipples. It was livid.

As he soaped himself up, Mister Bob became aware of the not-quite-white noise of the extractor fan. He was surprised to notice it at first because the sound was ever-present and he, like anyone probably, had a natural tendency to "tune out" ever-present sounds. Even so, it was odd that he hadn't noticed it before now since the noise was so off-white. The blade inside it was catching on something each time it went around.

Mister Bob wondered why this should be. He had never knowingly knocked or bumped or tried to adjust the plastic housing around the extractor fan. He was at a loss as to what could have caused the internal fan blade to start catching. Things fall apart, he supposed. It was a law of thermodynamics. He was no stranger to things falling apart.

Mister Bob tried to ignore the extractor fan and its slightly catching blade.

Mister Bob closed his eyes and thought of vast libraries of books, but he could still hear the catching blade and, more annoying than the noise of the blade itself, were cyclical thoughts about the mystery of *how* it could be catching. It was gnawing at him now, catching on his consciousness like, well, like an extractor fan blade impossibly caught on something, slightly but nevertheless irritatingly. It was like an itch.

In the way that someone who can't sleep at night, despite all the comforts of a good bed, might take to counting sheep behind their eyelids in the hopes of flushing out the unwanted insomniac visions, Mister Bob tried to name as many characters as possible from Stendahl's *Le Rouge et le Noir*. It had been two weeks since he had finished the last page and closed the book. There was Julien Sorel, of course, the leading man in all of this. But there was also:

Abbé Chélan, the wise priest.

The Marquis of Mole. Mister Bob had not forgotten that name.

There was Madame Rênal of course.

Um.

There was Fouqué, the fellow with the sawmill and the mountain retreat.

Ah.

Was that it? Had Mister Bob had spent the best part of a month munching through this great classic in between stints of cleaning seat-back trays only to recall the names of five of its many, many characters?

No. Because there was also *Old* Sorel, Sorel's dad. And, ah, um, there was a Russian Prince in it as well, he thought. Half a point for a Russian Prince.

Mister Bob was annoyed with himself. He opened his eyes and they were met by the clicky extractor fan.

He tried to think instead of literary bathtubs. There was Mencken's fictional history of the bathtub, of course. And Sam Shepard's play. Oh, and Enderby! Mister Bob hadn't thought of Mister Enderby in years. Mister Enderby in those novels by Anthony Burgess was a suffering poet who had written poetry while sitting on the toilet. And when he'd written or half-written a poem, he would toss it into the bathtub next to him. Enderby's bathtub had served essentially as a slob's filing cabinet and had been overflowing with paper and scraps of food and, eventually, rats. Mister Bob's had been full of bits and bobs too: unused cleaning products and thrown-aside old toothbrushes mainly. He felt at one for a moment with Mister Enderby. It wasn't a great feeling.

Ah.

He knew there was mention of bathtubs, "hot baths" specifically, in the *Iliad* but no matter how hard he cudgelled his brains, Mister Bob could not remember how or why that should be. He could remember Pooter though. From *Diary of a Nobody*. Pooter had found some red paint he liked and had gone around his house, The Laurels of course, painting things red. One of his victims had been the bathtub, which he painted red inside and out. Later, when bathing, the red paint came away and Pooter was left sitting in a bath of what he momentarily thought was his own blood. It was a funny book.

Um.

The Shining? Did someone have a bath in Stephen King's *The Shining*? Mister Bob couldn't remember. It wasn't his sort of thing. The *Iliad* was supposedly his sort of thing though. If only he could remember the bathtubs of antiquity in the *Iliad*...

THAT BLOODY FAN!, thought Mister Bob, *I mean, it's not even taking in any steam!* His bathwater was once again tepid and producing no steam. The mirrors were completely unfrosted.

Sod it all.

Mister Bob swam forward to capture the shower head, which sat on a little brass fixture like a dainty telephone receiver. He turned the tap marked "H" to the on position and water gushed forth. It was cold but he convinced himself that a spray of cold water in a hot bath would be like something from one of those Scandinavian or even Ancient Roman spas. He flipped the little switch that channelled the water from the main tap to the shower head and cold water fizzed out through the rose.

Once the water fizzing satisfyingly from the shower head reached a temperature slightly north of freezing, Mister Bob turned the shower head on himself.

After shooting the pupils and teachers, he turned the gun on himself.

Mister Bob wasn't sure what made him think of that and it certainly gave him a start.

Knock-knock-knocking on Heaven's door...

He shook himself out of it and remained glad that a mere phrase had run though his head like a strip of tape rather than a full-blown Panic Vision. Mister Bob had enjoyed a relatively long period of being untroubled by the Visions and he hoped they would not come back. He squinted in suspicion at the extractor fan again. Its success at mildly irritating him with its catching fan blade had almost caused his imagination to start acting without permission again.

Never mind, thought Mister Bob, *it doesn't matter.*

He ran the lukewarm shower water over his chest and collar bone and then under his arms. It turned back to cold again suddenly but it felt good and refreshing. Mister Bob picked up the LOTUS FLOWER soap bar and smelled it, flaring his nostrils widely to capture as much of its vapour as possible. It too felt good and he could feel himself becoming less fraught, could feel himself *coming down*, unwinding.

Mister Bob remembered why he had turned the shower on and then used it to wash his hair with some Superdrug shampoo. It occurred to him for the first time that there would no doubt be fancy, fine-smelling shampoos he could buy too. There were so many things out there to aid the balding, formerly-stinking 54-year-old man in his bathtime.

It was all expensive for what it was of course, but this prompted him to reflect on the unique modern stinginess around things like bathing. First of all, people didn't *bathe* anymore at all. People took showers. Showers were supposedly more efficient, used less water, less energy, less time. But what was so wrong about using plenty of those resources in service of wellness? What had happened to simple, accessible luxury? It seemed to Mister Bob that people didn't want it. The people of the United Kingdom had become misers, maybe always were misers. Not just misers of money, but misers of the soul. They had become spiritual misers, like something from Stendahl. Stendahl was French though, so it was worse for Mister Bob because spiritual miserliness in Britain was made manifest as pissy carpets around the bases of toilets, and boilers filled with limescale that made water only tepid, and extractor fans that met a legal requirement but didn't actually draw any steam from the room, and, ah, um, hopeless grey dust down the backs of radiators. God save the Queen.

Nothing less than all-out Revolution was required, thought Mister Bob. His would be a Revolution of the spirit and, yes, he really felt this, it had already begun. He had started it himself, here, in this bathtub, surrounded by livid pink Best-of-British fungus.

It hadn't been his idea. It had been Tracey's. And she hadn't used genius to come up with it, but merely let him into a living secret. Women hadn't given up on baths. Women had been keeping the soul alive. It was the men of this stinking country, Mister Bob saw clearly now, who had led the eager descent into spiritual miserliness. They couldn't have their little Empire anymore so they would wreck themselves through a sort of starvation instead. It was a spiritual hunger strike, petulant and unending. It was all perfectly clear now, to Mister Bob, here in the bathtub.

Anyway, didn't people tend to shower at least once a day? When Mister Bob had been growing up, a bath was a weekly event while *Songs of Praise* was on, yes? So was a daily shower, quick and managerial, really any more economical than a luxurious weekly glug in the tub? And who cared about efficiency anyway? Wasn't there enough hot water to go around now that everyone had one of these combination boilers? Efficiency! Who *cared*? Mister Bob, surrounded now by his fine-smelling soaps and reunited with his old sailing friend Mister Matey, did not care.

It was a new one on Mister Bob, this "not caring" business. And he *did* not care. He didn't care about whether his life was half-over or not, he didn't care about the gingivitis or athlete's foot since he knew they were only temporary, he didn't care about being repellent through stench since he no longer was. Mister Bob certainly didn't care if the plastic blade inside his extractor fan was catching on something. Fuck it.

Mister Bob rinsed the shampoo out of his hair (Had it thinned any further? He didn't care all of a sudden) and the soap from the rest of his body. It smelled wonderful. *He* smelled wonderful.

Mister Bob whistled a little tune.

Wheet-wheet-wheeetle-wheet-wheetie-wheeeeet!

Surprised by how it reverberated against the tiled walls and the twin mirrors and perhaps also the ceramic-like materials of the bathtub and the wash basin and the toilet bowl, Mister Bob whistled louder.

Wheet-wheet-wheeetle-wheet-wheetie-WHEEEET!

And then he sang the lyrics to the tune that had been going around in his head for what seemed like months on end.

"Knock-knock-knockin' on Heaven's Door...!"

Mister Bob submerged himself fully, came back up with a mouthful of soapy bathwater, gargled loudly, and then spat it out like a cartoon fish. "YEAH!" he sang out loud, enjoying the bathroomly reverberations for their own pure sake.

Nobody banged the wall or ceiling in an unneighbourly way. Nobody came knocking at *his* door this time. Nobody minded what Mister Bob was up to in his bathtub even if it happened to be Revolution.

★

As fun as all the echoey singing was, Mister Bob took a mental note to find out how to play music when in the bathtub. He remembered his mother dragging a large radio into the bathroom as a way to enjoy her own soaks in the tub, the long electric cable trailing dangerously from a plug socket in another room by means of an extension cord. Nobody gave a hoot for safety in the '60s, did they? He'd try to work something out with his dratted mobile phone.

Mister Bob tried to relax more mindfully using only internal resources and felt himself drifting off. He knew not to actually fall asleep though. For all his thoughts of self-termination, he had no desire to forget his whereabouts today and to slip beneath the soap-greyed water.

He felt himself thinking of *Don Quixote*, perhaps recalling the wind turbines he increasingly saw from train windows. First, he imagined himself as the Knight of the Sorrowful Countenance and then, more realistically perhaps, he imagined himself as Sancho Panza. Then, he changed the scale of these adventures and found himself imagining a Body Gnome version of *Don Quixote* playing out on his soapy stomach, the Knight and his squire sallying forth hopelessly into the bottomless pit of his bellybutton. "Tally-ho!" *Plumf!*

After another twenty minutes, the water was starting to cool but Mister Bob did not yet want to get out of the bathtub. Instead, he lay back as far as he could and looked up at the ceiling. He felt the water tickling the underside of his chin.

He hadn't looked up at a ceiling for any prolonged amount of time since he was a boy. He used to go to bed at 7 o'clock because that was his prescribed bedtime but he was never ready to sleep. Instead, he would stare up at the ceiling and look for shapes in the soft artex. He tried to do that now with Mrs. Cuntapples' bathroom ceiling but its artex wasn't craggy enough and nothing would come. The ceiling of his childhood bedroom had been deeply nuanced in its cragginess. Since no new images were forthcoming, Mister Bob remembered some of the old ones. The memories were easy to catch in his relaxed state.

The first ceiling shape he could remember was a sort of raccoon-looking creature. In fact, it seemed to be part raccoon and part skunk. A raccunk. This had been his favourite one, he remembered, his best soft artex ceiling friend.

To the raccunk's right, or to its "east" since the ceiling suggested a relief map, had been a real prehistoric scene. God, he hadn't thought of this in decades. A giant land crab battled with a dinosaur-looking creature while another dinosaur—a female, he had decided—looked on fretfully. The two male monsters had been battling ferociously for the female one. It struck Mister Bob now as an immensely dramatic scenario for a small boy to concoct while he was trying to sleep and quite a complex thing to see in the crags and contortions of a soft artex ceiling. But he remembered it well.

There had also been something he'd called A Cracky Monster, a sort of turd-looking or log-like creature with a troubled human face. The look on its face seemed to be saying "kill me!" Right from the depths of the frustrated preconscious mind that one, Mister Bob supposed. He realised that A Cracky Monster was the sort of thing he might witness in a future Panic Vision now that he had remembered it.

Mister Bob tried to put the thoughts of his old ceiling friends out of his mind for the time being. Instead, he looked at his fingertips, which had become wrinkled. This was nostalgic to him too: his mother had called them "raisin fingers" and said that if he spent too long in the bathtub he would "turn into a prune."

What horrors there were in childhood. Bed at 7. Prehistoric battle scenarios. Cracky Monsters. Children transforming unwittingly into sun-dried fruits.

Even as a fully-grown man, Mister Bob didn't want to turn into a prune.

He sighed resignedly. It was time to get out of the bath.

Intermission

Pavel stood at the door of the flat, a fingergrubbed number 7 at his eye level, and rummaged surreptitiously in his trouser pocket for the key.

He'd taken it upon himself to cut his own copy one afternoon. He'd found that Mister Bob had left his keys in the door while he was out at work and so Pavel had taken the forgotten key to the Timpsons inside the Morrison's supermarket in Portobello town centre. He'd had copies cut of both the mortise and Yale locks ("yes, it is the key to my home!" he'd told the Timpsons man), and then put Mister Bob's originals safely back where he'd found them.

Before opening the door today, Pavel splayed the letterbox open with two fingers and peeped inside. Since his knowledge of train schedules was perfect, he had a good idea that Mister Bob would not be home, but he liked to check. He could usually get a sense of the flat's unoccupied silence by peeking inside and looking for moving shadows. Satisfied by the sense of stillness in the giant's absence, Pavel opened the door and the usual soul-warming smell of books tumbled out upon him.

Mister Bob's flat was pathologically full of books but Pavel did not think anything of it one way or another. Mister Bob worked on the Marvellous Caledonian Sleeper and this enchanted Pavel. He wanted to know what sort of man could be given such wonderful, satisfying work. Pavel idolised Mister Bob.

As usual, the first thing to meet Pavel's gaze on entering the flat was the impossible amount of junk mail littering the floor. There were fast food menus and special offer circulars from supermarkets. He wasn't sure why Mister Bob didn't just put them in the recycling bin like everyone else. After all, you had to separate it from the regular morning post; you'd have it in your hands and you'd have to *choose* to drop it on the floor. It didn't make a lot of sense to Pavel whose own flat was as neat as a station master's office.

Beyond the ocean of junk mail was the bathroom where, he noticed, something was different but he couldn't quite see what that might be. A light floral aroma hung in the air.

Pavel continued into Mister Bob's bedroom. The bedroom held yet more books. As well as the book-lined walls and books placed in higgledy-piggledy or helical stacks atop of a chest of drawers and what used to be a dressing table, Mister Bob had constructed a sort of balcony over his bed. It looked almost like the canopy above a four-poster bed but was solid like a shelf and contained ever more books. He must have slept fitfully beneath its great weight like a submariner might sleep beneath the weight of the ocean.

Most of Mister Bob's books looked secondhand but some of them had beautiful oxblood or gold-coloured spines. Pavel knew this to be remarkable but books didn't particularly interest him. His was a different anorak mania.

Pavel sat upon Mister Bob's unmade bed. He peeped beneath the sheets and marvelled at the grot within. The once-white fitted sheet that covered the mattress was saggy and clearly intended for a larger-sized bed than this one, bought in impatient haste and, if the stains were anything to go by, several years ago.

The underside of the balcony was latticed with a cacophony of paper keepsakes wedged into the slats. There were beer mats displaying the emblems of Innis & Gunn, West, Tetley, John Smith's, Babycham, Holden's, Banks's bitter; checkout receipts from W. H. Smith, Blackwell's of Edinburgh, Jarndyce Books, Clarks shoes, Big Boy Shirts Ltd., BABISH, Lush soaps; and a picture postcard of the International Space Station against a backdrop of starry outer space. Pavel had noticed the picture postcard before and it puzzled him. It was anomalous. Mister Bob did not otherwise seem concerned with technology or space, so it was odd that he should sleep directly beneath an image of humanity's greatest achievement in terms of technology and international cooperation. Hope maybe? Did the ISS represent hope to Mister Bob? Or maybe an office among the stars was just a pleasant thing to dream about? Pavel did not know.

Pavel picked up Mister Bob's pillow, wrapped it around his face and inhaled deeply.

"Ah, Mister Bob," said Pavel and he savoured the familiar earthy, fructuated, root vegetable scent.

Sometimes, Pavel would continue to sit here, on Mister Bob's bed, and merrily tug one out, but he had no time today. His friend Lorraine from the Trainspotters' Club was coming to visit at any moment and they would continue their discussion of 1920s English and Welsh signal boxes. Lorraine was a real connoisseur and she had much to teach Pavel on the subject. They would usually have a glass of wine to drink and conversations could become somewhat spirited before she noticed the time and had to head back to Waverley for the 17:22 to Pennycruik where she lived with her husband. Lorraine's husband was called Colin and he owned a telescope. Pavel found astronomy to be the height of crackpot nerdery but it took all kinds to make a world.

Pavel went into the bathroom again and noticed the four soaps, two of which were festively coloured and one of which looked like a chunk of coal and one of which was a more regular creamy white. They were all shiney with water so Mister Bob must have used all four quite recently. This struck Pavel as a lot of soap for one man and he wondered if Mister Bob had found a girlfriend at last. Well, he deserved it. Pavel felt happy for Mister Bob. As if to celebrate their union, Pavel licked each bar of soap and then went to examine the living room.

The living room, like the bedroom and entry hall, was lined with old books. Some of them had Latin or Greek-looking titles on the spines and Pavel didn't understand their meaning at all. Where he had grown up, Latin text was not uncommon to see on public buildings, but it had never meant much to him. He had moved to the UK as soon as he was able in order to enjoy the railway lines laid down during the Industrial Revolution. All countries had wonderful train systems of course but there was something about these plucky British ones under slate Victorian skies that made Pavel's soul sing.

On the table, next to seven empty beer bottles (*naughty-naughty, Mister Bob!*) was Mister Bob's work schedule. This was what Pavel had been looking for. Secret snorkings of Mister Bob's pillow and tastings of his bathroom soap collection were wonderful but merely bonuses. Most train enthusiasts could only examine and commit to memory the officially published train timetables, but a railway company employee's work schedule could offer a glimpse into a whole other *system*. Systems were the key to railway enthusiasm. Pavel liked systems.

The top left-hand corner of the work schedule displayed the sans-serif logo of the railway company while the bottom right-hand corner displayed the signature of Mister Bob's manager. Pavel pressed Sunny's signature with his thumb as if it were a talisman and then he marvelled at the numbers—the times and platforms and train registrations—that told Pavel a story.

The details of Mister Bob's work week now committed to memory, Pavel made his way back through the sea of junk mail and into the stairwell, what locals called "the close" for reasons he did not know, and closed the door softly behind him. He turned the key in the lock and returned it to his pocket. Pavel pressed his fingerprints to the brass number 7, chuckled to himself, and went back to his flat to prepare the spread of white wine, poached eggs and pickled onions for the visit from Lorraine.

December

Five

Mister Bob already wore his polyester railway company uniform as he rested against the counter in the skinny, corridor-like kitchen. He'd been squawked awake by a seagull five minutes before the alarm clock was due to go off, but he found himself in a serene mood nonetheless. Now, he was having breakfast: listening to the kitchen radio while savouring the antigravity sensation of eating a boiled egg.

Mister Bob had worn his tie long today for the first time. He had taken the time to finally work it out in front of the bathroom mirror.

It was Monday morning and the unreasonable winter sunshine blared through the window at the end of the kitchen as if beckoning Mister Bob prematurely to the afterlife.

Mister Bob had two stupidly long days ahead of him, but he felt extremely good about it for reasons he could not put his finger on.

Everything was fine.

And even if it wasn't fine later, if the day's fineness ran out somehow, Mister Bob was in the here-and-now and enjoying his breakfast egg. The future couldn't be predicted and, as such, it didn't matter.

"This is the 6Music News at seven o'clock" chirped the radio, "with me, Katherine Cracknell..."

"No thank you!" said Mister Bob, snapping the radio off.

Why did they need to have hourly news broadcasts on a radio station purportedly devoted to music? There must be something Reithian to it, a commitment for BBC output to "inform, educate, *and* entertain" and that a station of pure music wouldn't meet the minimum criteria for all of those promises. But if it was so important to honour all three, why didn't they have an hourly broadcast of avant-garde jazz on BBC Parliament?

He decided not to worry about it. Instead, Mister Bob regarded the eggcup from which he scooped his egg. He could not remember buying it or otherwise acquiring it. It must have come with the flat. This struck Mister Bob as strange. He did not remember the TO LET advert saying "fully furnished with telephone lines, combination boiler, bath mat, and egg cups. Carpeted throughout."

"Yes, Mrs. Buntapples," he did not recall saying on

the phone, "I am interested in the facilities but the egg cups were what really caught my attention. Perhaps I could view them on Saturday afternoon?"

None of this came to him as a Vision but Mister Bob remained alert to any advance warnings of Visions; warnings like sweat, for example, erupting suddenly from his armpits like the inky panic of a squid. He had, after all, two long days ahead of him. The journey for which Mister Bob was now preparing looked like this: he'd take the 124 bus from Portobello Town Hall to Waverley Station as usual, then he would take the 07:27 from Waverley to Dundee. He would then stay overnight in Dundee, during which time he planned to enjoy a full-blown drinking spree from 8:42am. On Tuesday, he would take the 18:55 from Dundee to Inverness, arriving at 21:28 with a short break before beginning his sleeper shift to London Euston. That was the plan. It was a good plan.

Mister Bob swallowed a piece of the egg and it made him feel as though he might float up to the ceiling.

Mister Bob's kitchen, or rather the kitchen in the flat that Mister Bob rented from Mrs. Cuntapples, was not the ideal kitchen for a fat man. It was almost as bad as the corridors of the sleeper train, only he had to dodge protuberant cabinet knobs instead of passengers' sticking-out parts.

Mister Bob spooned the last scrapings of egg into his mouth, tossed the ravaged shell into the pedal bin, and placed the rented egg cup in the sink. He then patted the pockets of his polyester railway company uniform to check that he had his keys and wallet and a couple of cigarettes.

Mister Bob did not usually smoke cigarettes but he sometimes found, after drinking a lot, that he might like one. Trying to find a corner shop in a drunken condition or, worse, asking strangers on the street for a cigarette was not very dignified for a moustachioed 54-year-old bachelor, especially one who was wearing a polyester railway company uniform. Mister Bob had learned this the hard way and now he always made sure he had a couple of loose cigarettes before leaving the flat. He favoured Lucky Strikes because he liked the design of the packet but, in practice, tended to place the cigarettes loose in his jacket pocket.

Mister Bob did not find any cigarettes in his jacket pocket but, in their place, he found two packets of aspirin tablets. There was one packet in each pocket.

He remembered now that he'd bought one packet of aspirin tablets at BABISH when he'd felt obliged to buy something. And then he'd bought a second packet in the Superdrug. Why had he done that? Well, he'd been embarrassed about the Mister Matey Bubble Bath. The cashier had probably imagined he'd got some sort of child trap in mind. Or else some terrible case of arrested development. The truth was that he'd wanted to reignite the pleasure of youthful bathtime memories, but that would have been hard to explain to a judgemental cashier with a nose piercing and whose eyebrows were tattooed on. The gulf between them in terms of life experience had just been too vast.

The cashier in the Superdrug had not worn a nose piercing, nor had her eyebrows been tattooed on. His review of this past event was being augmented in the present by his mildly racing imagination. He was not even aware of this. To Mister Bob, the Superdrug cashier *had* worn a nose ring and her eyebrows *had* been tattooed on. Mister Bob lived half in reality and half in fantasy, even on relatively clear-headed days like this one.

Mister Bob took both packets of aspirin tablets from his pockets and placed them on the kitchen counter and then he did something very odd.

Mister Bob opened one of the kitchen cabinets, the one above the toaster, and produced his "prison."

Mister Bob's "prison" was based on that thing Scotch Gran had done when he was a boy: the instant coffee jar with parchment paper stretched over the top as a makeshift piggy bank for twenty-pence pieces. Mister Bob did not collect twenty-pence pieces. His prisoners instead were aspirin tablets and he had accumulated at least half a coffee jar's worth. He was saving them for his suicide.

Where it had once felt inevitable, the only plausible exit from his general turmoil, Mister Bob had not seriously considered ending his life for quite a while. In fact, he felt almost surprised to be looking at the prison jar now. The bathtime soaks had shown him that life could be improved. He'd been glistening.

Frequent soaks in the bath had stopped Mister Bob from stinking of root vegetables but they had also, through the simple acts of filling his nostrils with herbal aromas and relaxing his shoulder muscles with hot water and casting his mind back to the good times of childhood, made it clear to Mister Bob that there were other ways of changing his consciousness and therefore getting out of trouble. He had already decided, from his bathtub, to Get Better.

He still believed in Getting Better and so the following actions were conducted in a zombie-like trance:

Mister Bob opened both packets of aspirin tablets and he dumped the cardboard packets into the kitchen pedal bin.

Mister Bob popped each aspirin tablet, one at a time, from the first blister pack and fed them into the prison through the slot in the parchment paper lid.

Mister Bob popped each aspirin tablet, also one at a time, from the second blister pack and fed them like those from the first packet into the prison through the slot in the parchment paper lid.

Mister Bob said the word "prisoners" with a sense of finality and in some sort of agreement with himself.

Mister Bob put the empty blister packs in the bin, dropping them on top of the cardboard packets, the shattered eggshell, and various other pieces of rubbish.

Mister Bob touched the top of the prison with the palm of his hand as if closing an imaginary lid.

Mister Bob put the prison back inside the kitchen cupboard, above the toaster. It sat discreetly next to a sticky jar of Marmite. All of the aspirin tablets were visible inside the jar and Mister Bob saw that they reached almost three-quarters of the way to the top.

Already enough to do the job, probably. It was a deathly, secret sight.

Snapping out of his mechanical zombie state, Mister Bob found himself perfectly cheerful, sufficiently recharged after a decent night's sleep, and looking forward to the private bender he'd be having in Dundee very shortly. He gave no further thought to aspirin tablets or to The End.

Mister Bob packed a small bag. He did not usually pack a bag for work trips, preferring to wear the only set of clothes he would need on his trip and leaving the business of tooth-brushing and other matters of personal hygiene until his return to Portobello. This, he realised, was probably why he had gingivitis and part of why he, until recently, had reeked.

Packing a small bag was part of Getting Better.

Mister Bob realised that he didn't own anything like an overnight bag. He only had a large brown leather suitcase that sat on top of his wardrobe, a position from which it watched him sleep like a squatting succubus.

Somehow, Mister Bob didn't feel like lugging the demon suitcase around Scotland with him for forty-eight hours so he hunted through the carrier bags in a kitchen drawer, settling on the paper bag he had been given at Lush on Oxford Street.

He put the paper bag up to his face like he had before, covering his nose and mouth like a horse's nosebag and found that the bag still smelled of a combination of his soaps, SNOW FAIRY, LOTUS FLOWER, and GODDESS. He fancied he could also smell a trace of the wonderful LOVELY JUBBLIES that had made his body feel so firm and soft but that was probably his imagination at work since the LOVELY JUBBLIES had come in a plastic pot with a screw-on lid.

He placed the bag on his bed, which he had actually *made* for once as part of his campaign to Get Better, and placed inside it a clean t-shirt and a fresh pair of balled-up argyle socks.

Mister Bob marched stoutly into the bathroom, took his toothbrush from the pot on the wash basin, and selected the GODDESS soap, which had become his favourite, from the line-up of four soaps on the side of the bathtub. The fourth soap was his original, plain white military-style soap bar.

This fourth bar of soap looked gloomy and depressed and there was a hair on it.

Mister Bob picked up this relic and dumped it squarely into the bathroom bin.

Scanning around for other things to take on his journey, his eyes fell upon his sailor friend Mister Matey. Yes, he would take Mister Matey with him as a symbol of his Getting Better and also as a symbol of travel or adventure. Mister Bob didn't usually see these long train-based work shifts as "travel" and he certainly didn't see them as adventures but maybe a fresh and positive state of mind was what he needed. Wasn't that what this was all about? Mister Matey would come along for the ride. He would at once be a travelling companion, a sort of talisman, and maybe, if his Dundee hotel room happened to have a bathtub in it, he might prove useful as well. He put it all into the Lush bag on his bed.

He then opened his bedside drawer and selected a single condom from next to his handkerchieves. Mister Bob had long ago given up on the idea of enjoying sexual activity with anyone ever again but he had been feeling more optimistic of late.

He squinted at the expiry date on the little foil packet and saw that the date had passed by seventeen years. It was also one of the old-style condoms you didn't see anymore with the chewing gum-like format, almost certainly bought from a machine in a men's toilet in a pub somewhere. He couldn't remember where. Still, the chance of its needing to be deployed were remote and it would be better than nothing. At the very least, should he end up in somebody's company, he could look at the expiry date and say "oh, foo" instead of just saying "ah, um, I don't have a condom." Yes, it could serve as a prop in a little acting ritual if nothing else. Mister Bob put it in the bag. It hit Mister Matey in his perpetually smiling face.

And finally, a book. Mister Bob scanned the shelves above his bed. He had vowed to pack, on this occasion, something less socially deathly than a dense book by Stendahl or de Maistre or Balzac. If anyone on the train spoke to him and asked him what he was reading, he would feel less embarrassed if he took... yes... that

Viz annual he'd bought from the Smiths at Glasgow Central. *The Council Gritter*. A harmless comic book. Something for everyone. Mister Bob felt almost normal.

Mister Bob placed the book, bottom edge first, into the bag. It provided a nice bulkhead into which the other items could lean.

He took his keys and wallet from where he had thrown them on the living room coffee table, picked up the paper bag from its rectangular paper handles, and went out into the world.

"Hoy, Mister Bob!" called Pavel.

This time, Mister Bob had not got very far down the stairs. He had, in fact, only just left his flat and was in the process of turning the key in the mortise lock.

It was not often he left the flat so early, his shifts usually beginning late in the day. Perhaps the early start accounted for his good mood. If he was a Morning Person by nature he had not been granted many opportunities to discover it.

Perhaps Pavel was a morning person too, though what he had to get up for was hardly obvious.

"Good Morning Pavel," said Mister Bob.

"Haha," said Pavel, laughing at nothing and wagging his finger in a chiding way as if he had caught Mister Bob in the act of doing something criminally exciting, "Mister Bob, you are not working the sleeper today?"

Pavel had bad breath. Did Pavel's girlfriend tell him

that he reeked? Was Pavel on his own adventure of toothbrushing and artisanal dental floss? Mister Bob couldn't imagine. Pavel wasn't one for Getting Better: he was more one for Getting Away With It.

"What?" said Mister Bob, "Oh, no, I see what you mean. Well deduced, Pavel. But as a matter of fact..."

"You take the 7:27 from Waverley to Dundee..." said Pavel so correctly that it sent a shiver down Mister Bob's spine.

"Yes," said Mister Bob.

"...*via*," continued Pavel, "Haymarket, Kirkaldy, Leuchars, aaaaaand," he saved the final station stop as if it were the reveal of a magic trick or the punchline to a joke, "*Aberdeen*, haha!"

"How could you possibly know all of that?" asked Mister Bob, his mouth slightly ajar. He felt very prim all of a sudden, almost like an upstanding citizen in the face of this strange little man. He wondered if Pavel knew how to wear his tie at the socially-approved length.

"Well, Mister Bob," said Pavel gravely, "you must be catching the bus from here at City Hall to be leaving at this times and that means you catch a train from Waverley and that means only one of a few think. Dundee seemed most likely to moy and I be knowing the route like, how you say, back of your mother's hand."

"Remarkable," said Mister Bob because it was, in fact, remarkable. Mister Bob wondered if, perhaps, Pavel's psychotic magic could be useful. He had found himself at times semi-stranded at some unstaffed countryside railway station, unsure of next arrivals. Because he didn't understand the Internet, he always needed to call the railway company's information hotline, which involved being put on hold for stupidly long stretches of time even though he was a railway company employee and access to schedules would have improved his day and his ability to do his job no end. But if he could call Pavel…

No. Mister Bob didn't want to let Pavel into his life even to this extent. Mister Bob didn't dislike his neighbour but he felt he was one of those lonely people to whom you'd show a jot of affection and they'd be knocking on your door in the middle of the night asking for your help in lancing a boil.

Mister Bob didn't fancy it.

"You really know your trains," said Mister Bob for want of anything else to say, and then, because he had ample time to reach the bus stop for once, "I am, as it happens, working the Callie Sleeper tomorrow evening after an overnighter in Dundee."

He wondered if the word "overnighter" was too suggestive of his planned bender and that he'd inadvertently let Pavel into his private plan. His panic did not last long however because Pavel had something else on his mind.

"Oh, Mister Bob," said Pavel, "if you could bring me a something?"

"Of course," said Mister Bob, "in fact, I have something from my last shift that I had forgotten to give you."

Mister Bob fished in the pocket of his polyester

railway company uniform and felt a sheet of paper he couldn't remember placing in there and the circular bar of soap whose cellophane wrapper proudly displayed the regal Monarch of the Glen emblem, which he had indeed pocketed for Pavel but then forgotten about until now.

He pulled both items out into the morning light.

"Ah, Mister Bob, you remembered me after all!"

Evidently Pavel had been feeling overlooked. Mister Bob realised suddenly that Pavel had been actively waiting for something to plop through his letterbox, and probably at a very particular time too, given his near-spooky knowledge of the schedules. He suddenly felt very observed and he tightened his tie knot self consciously.

Mister Bob handed the bar of soap to a gleeful Pavel and began to unfold the piece of paper, unsure of what it could be. Perhaps he had thought to pocket a napkin with the same emblem or perhaps a timetable or something too.

It was a rather scrappy doodle of something instantly recognisable to schoolboys of all lands and could only be described as a spunking cock.

"Oh, haha, Mister Bob, what is this?!" laughed Pavel, "naughty-naughty!"

Blushing, Mister Bob re-pocketed the, ah, um, diagram, and said, "I'm not sure who put, ah, *that* in, um, there."

Pavel was still laughing but Mister Bob could tell he was more interested in retreating into his flat, presumably to stash the sleeper train souvenir soap bar in whatever magpie nest he had built from similar things Mister Bob had brought him in the past and, most bizarrely of all, would continue to bring him in the future.

"Thank you again, Mister Bob!" said Pavel, "and be watching out for prick-pockets!"

"Yes," said Mister Bob, "you're very welcome Pavel."

Mister Bob made his way down the stairs.

"I'm not sure," Mister Bob had said, "who put, ah, *that* in, um, there."

In fact, he was precisely sure who had put it in there. It could only have been one person. Tracey.

Tracey must have drawn the spunking cock and put it in Mister Bob's pocket on the night they got drunk together on premium strength lager on the bottom bunk of his cabin on the sleeper. He wasn't sure how she could have committed such a sleight of hand without him noticing but, then again, he had been somewhat drunk.

But hadn't she been drunker still? She'd been drunk before she'd even arrived at his kitchen cabinet-like door brandishing the six-pack they went on to guzzle together.

It must have happened when he was talking to Sunny, while Tracey had been hiding behind the door. Could that be so? Could Tracey have had the audacity to make the doodle and then slip it into his pocket while he was protecting her from a chewing out by Sunny?

As unlikely as it seemed, Mister Bob supposed it must be so. His jacket had been hanging on the door, so it *would* have been accessible to her.

As Mister Bob made his way down the street towards the bus stop, he marvelled at the cheekiness of it. Was this any way to treat a gallant knight while he was in the actual act of skewering dragons for you?

He didn't laugh out loud but he couldn't stop himself from smiling. Mister Bob was tickled.

Reading meaning into it was another matter though. Even though reading was the one thing Mister Bob was really any good at, he couldn't decipher the meaning of the spunking cock.

Was it, as he imaginatively hoped, a message, an invitation to sex? Or was it just pointless, absurdist hijinks? Unable to roll her eyes at him while Sunny was being officious, was this her way of calling their boss a dick head? Was it a souvenir of that night, which had been, after all, his birthday? A crude improvisation in lieu of a birthday card?

He settled on the last option. But he hoped against hope it was the first.

Mister Bob noticed the orange hair and triangle-shaped head of David McManaman from across the station concourse.

Normally, even though he quite liked David, he would skulk quickly towards his train or the station master's office in the hope of not being spotted by him. Mister Bob wasn't sure why he did this, but of course it was because he was shy. It was as simple as that. Shyness can slowly destroy a person, robbing them of opportunities one by one, and it was one of the many things that had been working to slowly destroy Mister Bob from both the inside and out. He wasn't sure if his shyness had been there at the beginning of his destruction or if it was a symptom of early attacks on him from school and work and all the rest of it.

This time, Mister Bob decided he would walk up to David McManaman and shake his hand firmly.

"Hello David," said Mister Bob, striding towards David McManaman and extending his hand.

David McManaman looked a bit panicked as Mister Bob approached. There was probably some part of David McManaman that thought this newly-assertive Mister Bob was going to produce a shotgun from somewhere and blow his head off with it.

"Oh, heh-heh," said David, "hello Bob."

Mister Bob noticed that David McManaman was holding two little white paddles for signalling that trains could leave. In the old days these would have been flags, he supposed. These paddles looked more like something designed for light sexual spanking.

Mister Bob squinted his eyes in resistance to the obvious Panic Vision that might come tearing into his mind but it didn't come. David McManaman must have noticed the pained expression on Mister Bob's face because he said "wha's wrang with ya, Bob?"

"Oh, ah, nothing, um, David," said Mister Bob, "just a touch of the belly blight."

Mister Bob patted his tummy and smiled in what he hoped was a benign manner.

"Well as long as it's nothing serious," said David, "are you arf to the Sneck?"

"Dundee first. I'll be working a shift up to Dundee. I've agreed to a trolley service. And then it's to the Sneck tomorrow."

"Dundee is it?" said David, "well-well."

There was an awkward silence as neither bachelor could think of anything to say next. It was difficult having nothing to say when Mister Bob had marched so purposefully up to David from all the way across the concourse.

"Ah," said Mister Bob, "where can I find, um, a trolley?"

Mister Bob already knew where the train stewards collected their tea trolleys at Waverley. It was a famous place to anyone who worked for the railway company. He only asked the question so that he could break the silence.

"Over at the trolley bay," said David McManaman, and he pointed the way with one of his spanking paddles in a way that suggested he'd rather be playing table tennis.

"Thanks," said Mister Bob, "I'll see you later."

"See you later, Bob," said David McManaman.

And that was that.

"Give that tart Tracey one from me!" called David across the criss-crossing of commuters in their H&M office casual.

A weak "I will!" was all Mister Bob could manage but his voice cracked and he wasn't sure it had landed.

It really was a feeble "I will!" and Mister Bob wondered if he'd be able to call for help if he ever fell into the sea.

Mister Bob lived quite near to the sea. Falling into it and not being able to shout for help struck him as a real possibility. It gave him something to shudder about as he walked across the station concourse but he resisted the Panic Vision that threatened to rise up.

It wasn't that Mister Bob lacked the lung power for shouting but he did lack the confidence. He imagined weakly shouting for help while the tide washed him further and further out to sea, half-hoping that the message wouldn't be received by a lifeguard's ear for reasons he wasn't really sure of. He knew he wouldn't *want* to die in the ocean in such a stupid and pointless way but there was something inexplicably embarrassing about the signal successfully reaching its intended destination. Mister Bob wasn't sure if there was anything that could be done about such hopeless, potentially deadly shyness. Audibly calling for help wasn't exactly something you could practise at home.

Mister Bob arrived at the trolley bay.

Mister Bob tried to dispel thoughts of drowning

from his mind. In doing so, it occurred to him that drowning had become a theme in his nightmares and his Panic Visions and now even his idle imaginings. There was the strange vision of the plunge pool into which he might fall and drown in pain. There was the fleeting idea of drowning, face-down in waterlogged fields. And now there was this daydream of being helplessly washed out to sea. Maybe these were all premonitions and Mister Bob really would drown in his bathtub, his newfound sanctuary, after gobbling all of his imprisoned aspirin tablets. It struck Mister Bob as likely as his hands touched down the crash bar of a tea trolley.

The tea trolley was already stocked. This was normal. Standard procedure. There was a separate team of catering types who prepared the food and drinks for the trolley service. Mister Bob didn't know anyone on the catering team. Occasionally he'd see somebody in chef's whites and a little cardboard sailor hat not unlike Mister Matey's one, going out to smoke a cigarette by the bins at the back of major stations such as this one. But that was all. Thanks to twentieth century-style division of labour, the railway company catering team were vaguely mysterious, almost magical, to Mister Bob. They had their own ways and occupied their own world. Seeing one of them on a fag break was like spotting a fox at night. Or a Fraggle.

Mister Bob had almost forgotten. He was supposed to wear an apron for this job so he took one from a peg near the door of the trolley bay. He didn't particularly mind wearing an apron. These were the sort that wrapped around your waist and came down to your knees. Most people wouldn't even notice he was wearing it, but the idea was to instil a sort-of old-fashioned trolley dolly modality in the train car staff.

Mister Bob wrapped the apron around his waist. The pinafore strings dangled foolishly behind him.

Why the people on the catering team should wear chef's whites was unclear. They were anything but chefs. The food on the trolley amounted to little more than Kit-Kat Chunkies and Polo mints and shrink-wrapped flapjacks; the sort of confectionery and industrially produced junk you'd buy in a crap corner shop. There was no cooking involved. There was, however, an urn of boiled water on each trolley for making tea and instant coffee. But the trolley dolly, in this case Mister Bob, was responsible for that part. It struck Mister Bob that the closest thing to cooking in this entire process was not actually done by the catering team at all.

This was all by the by. As he pulled his trolley out of the bay and made his way towards Platform 7 for the Dundee train, Mister Bob idly wondered if he'd ever eat his aspirin tablets, if he'd ever take his own life. It had long felt inevitable but, lately, it was beginning to feel like unnecessary drama. He was, after all, Getting Better. Maybe he'd chuck them out.

Mister Bob whistled "Getting Better" by The Beatles as he and the trolley neared the platform.

The train was already at the platform and Mister

Bob produced his railway company staff card from his wallet and used it to pass through the ticket barrier. A ticket barrier-monitoring member of station staff in a high-vis vest gave Mister Bob a nod. He did not know Mister Bob but the trolley and the fact that he'd magically opened the ticket barrier by himself proved that Mister Bob was a colleague of sorts. Mister Bob wondered if the station staff saw him and the other railway company employees in the same way he saw the catering staff: uniquely different and obliquely mysterious, a fleeting glimpse being the sort of event you might want to wish upon like a shooting star. Probably not.

Mister Bob made his way along the platform to the door at the very end of the train and he stopped to pull the polyester from out of his arse crack.

Mister Bob also scratched his head for a moment while he tried to remember how to get the trolley onto the actual train.

Ah yes. The ramp.

Mister Bob produced the trolley-and-wheelchair ramp from behind a Victorian pillar decorated with wrought iron thistles and other intricate Scotchery.

He folded it open, deftly avoiding the sinister nip of a blood blister. He then wondered if the avoidance of a blood blister signalled the beginnings of an excellent shift or if it had squandered his allotted portion of luck for the day, if not the whole trip.

Mister Bob sighed the sigh of the perpetually fatigued.

But then he remembered he was Getting Better and he continued to whistle his tune as he heaved the trolley up the ramp.

He sensed the water sloshing in the urn and he hoped it would not inexplicably explode in his face, turning his most visible skin into cellophane, prompting a little kid passenger to point and laugh and say "haha, silly man!" and then their parent to say, "yes, Billy, a very silly man!" before turning to Mister Bob's wrecked face and saying, "do us decaf macchiato please, mate."

The business of being a trolley dolly was decidedly dull. Few people wanted trolley service these days because it was expensive and unnecessary. Most passengers on a given train would be doing a short hop of two or three stations and, as such, would not need food or drink. Other passengers just found it a waste of money. Two quid for a Kit-Kat was a bit silly. Three quid for a Mars bar was a fucking scandal.

It was also repetitive. You had to walk up and down the aisles, being careful not to smash the trolley off the armrests or skin someone's knuckles, saying "anything from the trolley? Anything from the trolley? Anything from the trolley?" over and over and over.

To entertain himself or at least to break up the monotony, Mister Bob found himself altering the emphasis on certain words in the phrase: "Would you like anything from the trolley? / "Would *you* like anything from the trolley?" / "Would you *like* anything from the trolley?" and so on. A favourite became "Would you like anything from *the* trolley?" because it was so absurd.

Sometimes, asking if they would like anything from the trolley could induce a kind of trance. This would often mean that the trolley dollies would miss someone saying "me please!" or "two teas!" and just zombie along, saying "anything from the trolley?" to everyone and no one until they crashed into the door of the driver's cabin.

This didn't usually happen to Mister Bob because he was so infrequently on trolley duty. He would surely hear every order. Mister Bob made an excellent trolley dolly. That is, if you overlooked the way his side flab rubbed along every aisle seat and sometimes folded people's ears back.

Mister Bob remembered something wonderful Tracey had told him. Tracey was mainly a cleaner and rubbish collector on the trains but she had done her time on the trolley service too.

Tracey said that she'd learned to fart silently in the faces of passengers who had pissed her off.

Once, when a man had given her a salacious wink, she'd vowed to get even. On her way back down the aisle, she'd paused slightly ahead of the offending passenger's seat and bent as if to busy herself with something on a low shelf of the trolley. She ensured that her arse was level with the man's face and then silently released a barrel of bum gas.

Tracey's bum gas, she had told Mister Bob, had come out silently but scentedly and was guaranteed to reach the nostrils of the idiot winker. He would have known it was deliberate and that there was nothing he could do about it. Revenge!

Mister Bob had laughed heartily at this story. It was the sort of story that made working on the trains worthwhile and Tracey had told it with her usual bawdy queen panache. He was delighted that Tracey had achieved her honking revenge but, secretly, he had also felt jealousy. The jealousy simmered in his guts like a revolting mustard-gassy stew.

That fart, Mister Bob felt, had been wasted on that passenger. Mister Bob sorely wished to have smelled one (just one!) of Tracey's farts.

Mister Bob dreamed of Tracey willfully farting in his face.

Mister Bob felt a stiffening in his polyester railway company trousers. Oh dear.

He idly opened and closed the brake on the trolley's back wheel and looked around at the various oily skidmarks on the vestibule carpet and felt himself wilting again. Phew.

Another thing Tracey had told him about getting revenge on passengers was to walk through the aisle with an open bin bag, asking for their rubbish. But instead of saying "your rubbish, your rubbish," you could say, "you're rubbish, you're rubbish, you're pieces of rubbish."

Mister Bob wished Tracey would repeatedly call him rubbish. But in a nice way.

★

When Mister Bob's lunch break rolled around, he felt that he deserved it. He wasn't used to all this trolley pushing, nor was he used to speaking to so many people who spoke to him rudely.

Since this wasn't the sleeper, Mister Bob would have to spend his break either talking to his colleague in the buffet cart or crammed into one of the available passenger seats. He chose the latter. In Quiet Coach F, he stuffed himself into a two-seat unit and watched the Lowlands slip by.

The train passed through some small towns built with mediaeval stone and Mister Bob was struck by how lovely it all was, how miraculous that such old buildings could still be permitted to stand in the age of whizzbang pocket supercomputers.

When he was small—and sometimes more recently too—Mister Bob had often imagined himself living in a stone house in the countryside. Most of the adults in his life lived in houses, often quite nice ones in the countryside. Today, however, it was difficult to get one. He wondered idly what had changed but it was the sort of questioning that threatened to become circular and lead to a Panic Vision. Mister Bob at least had a nice flat to rent and it was only one bus ride from the city centre and only three inconvenient travel connections from his main employment and he only needed to work one full-time job to pay for it.

A small room and a new book every couple of weeks without having to commute for hours on end in order to toil, also in motion, for even more hours on end, and Mister Bob would be happy. Well, not happy exactly. But it was the sort of arrangement that would quiet his pining for a quick and dispassionate death. And that was enough.

Except that had all changed recently, hadn't it? He'd been Getting Better. He'd been having ideas about change. Mister Bob had allowed his brain to squirt a smidgen of hope into itself. That was new. And he hoped now, on his lunch break, that it wouldn't all come tumbling down.

He closed his eyes and thought of hot baths. Apropos of this, he remembered the *Iliad* bathtub at last. Andromache, wife of Hector the conquering hero, orders her sexiest servants to prepare a hot bath to welcome her husband home from battle.

Little does she know that Hector is already dead.

"Poor woman," recited Mister Bob in bookish reverie, "she knew not that he was now beyond the reach of baths, and that Athena had laid him low by the hands of Achilles."

Pleased with the unconstipated and unexpected feat of memory, Mister Bob opened his eyes again. A swatch of neon colour peeked from the wire netting on the back of the seat in front of Mister Bob. It was a magazine. He plucked it from the netting so that he might idly flip through it in the absence of his Everyman edition of the *Iliad*.

Urgh, these lunch breaks. Though necessary for recuperation and for a few moments of privacy away from the Pepsi-demanding public, they held their own kind of awfulness. You were off the clock and theoretically free to do whatever you liked, but only within the confines of the workplace, which, in Mister Bob's case was a moving train and so he couldn't very well go anywhere. You could busy yourself with smalltalk or window-staring or mobile phone screen-jabbing or a small amount of book reading if you'd come prepared. But that was about it. And you couldn't take your eye off your wristwatch for long in case you missed your moment to swing back into tedious action. So in what way were you free at all? Mister Bob was being ripped off.

He looked at the cover of the magazine. It was intended for young women. Mister Bob was not a young woman. He was a balding, embarrassingly-moustachioed man. It felt transgressive even to touch it with his terrible unmanicured hands. But he hadn't *asked* to see the magazine. He hadn't walked into a train station W. H. Smiths to buy it like an unambitious pervert.

Mister Bob thumbed through the pages. It seemed to be mostly adverts for beauty products. A problem page was interesting though: a young woman was asking what she was supposed to do with her hands when kissing her boyfriend. She always felt awkward. Try putting your hands on his hips, the agony aunt helpfully suggested.

Mister Bob came to an article about something called self-care. At first, Mister Bob conflated this with "self-help," the kind of rubbishy books that told you the "rules" for life or how to live well or how to get ahead in your rubbishy white-collar career. But as he started to read, he realised quickly, self-*care* was something different.

These young women, it seemed, the intended readers of this magazine, were under a lot of pressure. They were expected to have thoughts and opinions about what struck Mister Bob as quite complicated political and interpersonal situations. They were also expected to pay off their student loans (Mister Bob learned from the magazine that many young people owed a breathtaking thirty thousand pounds or even more) and to have careers and to look adequately moisturised and epilated and made-up while doing it all. It struck him as so, so much.

The magazine article explained the importance then, "in this busy world," of self-care. Of taking time to yourself.

Finding the time to think about things other than your troubles and those of the world, the article explained, was good for you. It was good to meditate, to keep a journal, to experience wildlife or the stars, to be at peace. It mentioned something called ASMR, which Mister Bob did not understand.

What Mister Bob *did* understand, however, was the importance of retreat from the world when it got too much. Overwhelm was not a good state of mind. He wondered if "overwhelm" (which was the magazine's word, not Mister Bob's) and "toxicity" (also the magazine's word) were to blame for all the crazy Visions he'd had in his life. Mister Bob had always assumed there was something wrong with his brain but maybe it was a case of *toxic overwhelm*. He did not feel like dismissing the idea out of hand.

Mister Bob thought about the baths he'd been taking. He had not thought of them as "self-care" until now. It struck him now that they'd become *important* to him as self-care. He'd just lacked the terminology. He felt proud to have allowed himself such a thought, to have allowed himself such softness.

He imagined a baby being lowered gently, head supported by a motherly hand, into a small bathtub like he presumably once was.

But beware, the magazine article concluded, of commercial high street products sold on the promise of self-care. Sometimes, the magazine article explained, self-care is just an excuse for corporations to sell posh soap and bubble bath.

Humph, thought Mister Bob.

The sense of freedom that came from being in a city or town with no meaningful connection to the rest of his life was intoxicating. Mister Bob was in Dundee with over 24 hours to spare. It was the perfect environment for a drinking spree and he had planned it perfectly.

He usually started at a Wetherspoons, but because anything to do with Britain leaving the European Union made Mister Bob sick to his stomach, he had sworn off Wetherspoons for life.

It was a shame. Mister Bob had liked the old buildings—cinemas and banks usually—in which Wetherspoon pubs were usually situated. And he liked the cheap Real Ale that allowed him to get drunk without getting too hungover. But it was all closed to him now. He would never again sup the Leave voter's beer, so he went off to find some real pubs instead.

Mister Bob began at a pub near the train station. It was called, pleasantly, the Engine and Tender. He confidently asked for "a pint of your realest ale" and the bar maid didn't bat an eyelid at his awkwardness. She went immediately to a Green King IPA (not entirely real, Mister Bob supposed, but he had asked for "most" real and he took her at her word) and charged him four pounds and fifty pence. He took his pint to a table near the window where he could watch the railway commuters and eager shoppers going to and fro. He placed his Lush paper bag containing his spare socks and his toothbrush and whatnot by the side of his chair, taking from it his copy of *The Council Gritter*. He didn't plan to read it closely but it would serve as a prop in his performance as "normal human man." Mister Bob was more used to higher-brow literature, which is why he knew that Blaise Pascal had said that "all of humanity's problems stem from man's inability to sit quietly in a room alone."

Pascal, Mister Bob felt, was on the money. Why was it so difficult to just *sit*? Why did we need company all the time? Why do we futz about so much? Why did Mister Bob feel he had to busy himself in a book while on public transport?

As an experiment, he put the *Viz* annual back inside the paper bag by his feet. He left it half-sticking out though, a safety feature. He could whip it out and have it on the table top should the need arise.

A yellow-green poster sellotaped to the wall advertised a TRAIN ENTHUSIAST'S CLUB, every second Wednesday, here at the Engine and Tender. He wondered first about that apostrophe. And then he wondered if his neighbour Pavel ever came here. He didn't like the sudden and sobering possibility of a connection to his real life though, so he tried with a shiver to put the thought out of his head. Next time, he'd choose a pub further from the station.

Instead, Mister Bob looked out of the window and put some thought into the Pascal problem. Why was it so difficult just to *be*? He was immediately struck with an idea about how the discomfort of sitting still without doing anything was probably why so much art and culture and general industry existed in the first place. You might blame capitalism and the eternal grinding need to pay the rent on time but really, when it all came down to it, could it not be said that it was human nature to fidget?

He wasn't sure about this line of enquiry. Paying the rent really was important. Mrs. Cuntapples and her terrible glare were motivation enough for Mister Bob to keep riding the rails up and down the Pennines, saying good morning to Pavel and then hello to Babish again and again and again.

Mister Bob supped his Greene King IPA and decided to personalise the question. He couldn't answer anything about "all of humanity" since he felt so separated from it. Why, instead, couldn't he, Mister Bob, sit quietly in a room alone?

It was because he felt perverse.

Or not good enough.

Mister Bob felt like a wrong 'un.

He felt this way even though he hadn't done very much wrong at all. He paid his rent on time. He didn't let his alcohol problem affect anybody else. Mister Bob was a goodie.

But he felt like a piece of shit almost all of the time.

This was why he couldn't sit quietly alone in a room. Not out in public anyway. If someone was with him, he felt *vouched for*. Through their presence alone, a second person was essentially saying to the world, "don't worry, he's with me."

And if another person couldn't be with him, he'd have a book or some other activity to busy himself with. If he was busy instead of just present, he was sort-of vouched for by proxy. He may have been alone but he had an excuse. The world did not need to suspect him of deviance.

The world had done a real number on Mister Bob.

Mister Bob slurped his Greene King IPA again, the froth creaming up his moustache. In a minor triumph, he did not yet reach for his comic book. Instead, he reached for his mobile phone. There was something he wanted to look up.

The phone case was sweaty from being inside the pocket of his polyester railway company uniform trousers but he wiped it off with one of the paper napkins left triangularly on the table. He tapped in his access code—888888—and then grappled with chipolata fingers to get the browser to understand his commands.

First, he popped a word he'd been curious about into the dictionary app.

"Slang," it said, "the area between anus and testicles or vulva. So-named because it 'taint one thing or another."

Oh, thought Mister Bob, *the perineum. Why didn't anyone say so?*

Next, he ended up at something called "a tumbler site," though it was spelled "Tumblr." He'd remembered the web address from the magazine he'd found in the back-of-seat netting on the train. It was an example, the magazine had explained, of a new trend in "body positivity" and Mister Bob was treated to an endless stream of attractively-photographed, partially-nude fat women. And muscular women, women with scars, flat-chested women, tattooed women, hairy women, and a woman in surfer gear whose left foot had been chomped off by a shark. It was wonderful.

He looked around himself nervously. He didn't want anyone in the pub to glimpse the colours of exposed flesh on his phone screen and get the wrong idea. He wasn't perving.

What he saw was wonderful. Fat folds and dimples. Stretch marks and puckered belly buttons. He saw women proudly displaying their cellulite and their double chins. Their makeup, hair and what clothes they had on were soft, shimmery, and beautiful-coloured. They were right to be proud. They looked beautiful, desirable, confident. They looked like GODDESS smelled. He wanted to be like them.

Beneath each image was a string of appreciative and supportive comments from other women and from people fancying them. Mister Bob had rarely been given a supportive comment from another man or from people who fancied him. Maybe if he took some pictures and posted them somewhere like this? Was there a body positivity Tumblr thing for moustachioed 54-year-old men? If there was one that welcomed hairy women and amputees, he supposed there must be one out there somewhere.

After some clumsy scrolling and poking at the screen he found it. It was called The Bear Pit. And it was full of glittering blokes, just like him. He'd save that one for later.

Mister Bob thought back to the day he'd surveyed his own body in front of the mirror before his bath. He hadn't realised it at the time but it was the beginning of his own body positivity programme. He would seek to be more like the tumbling ladies as part of his campaign to Get Better. He'd be a happy "plus-size" man, always bathtub-fresh and mentally well.

Fuck it. Mister Bob felt good about himself today. What a productive day this had been already. A light breakfast and good feelings. A friendly hello with a familiar face at Waverley. And a paid journey to Dundee, a place of freedom, where he could now sup his pint like a free human being, ponder the big questions and make active headway into being positive about his bod.

There was a kerfuffle by the entrance to the pub and Mister Bob looked over to see what was the matter.

"Wehaaaaaaay!"

A horde of absolute lads had stormed the building like berserkers. One of them had a photograph of his own face printed on his t-shirt. It could mean only one thing: a stag do.

"Wehaaaaaaay!"

It's okay, thought Mister Bob as he felt his panic rise, *they are nothing to do with you. They will not notice you sitting here and pretending to read the Drunken Bakers in* Viz *while wondering about that Bear Pit.* He tucked his mobile phone back into his polyether railway company uniform trousers so that none of them would glimpse the exciting expanse of skin tones.

The berserker horde came right up to Mister Bob's table and slammed down a purple-coloured vodka jelly. They seemed to want him to drink it.

Mister Bob didn't want to be rude. Mister Bob was a goodie.

Six

Mister Bob was in a room-temperature bath and a flannel saturated with room-temperature water covered his eyes like a mask. The pain inside his head was intense, like opposing magnets were wrestling in there for impossible supremacy.

He tried to go over the events of the previous day (or had it been *today*?) but his brain rebelled. It couldn't face those events.

He had lost his Lush bag in the chaotic bender—all of his tidily-prepared things—and, he was fairly certain, he'd lost his clothes too.

He dearly hoped that when he could muster the courage, the completely insane bravado, to rise from the bathtub, he would find his polyester railway company uniform neatly folded by the side of the bed on which he had collapsed at some point and spent some time unconscious.

Or, if neatness and foldedness were too much to anticipate, perhaps he would find his clothes strewn between doorway and bed; a polyester railway company jacket here, some polyester railway company trousers there. That would be fine. Mister Bob had no idea what to expect.

How had he become involved with those awful people?

He had felt that he really couldn't say no to them. Perhaps the philosophical question Mister Bob had been pondering at the start of all this should not have been the one Pascal had asked but the one Sartre had asked about why we so often do things in bad faith. But no sooner had this idea occurred to him, the industrial pistons once again began pounding inside Mister Bob's head and he felt profoundly sick.

Why had the men come to him? He didn't know them from Adam. When he'd used this phrase to make sure this was not a case of mistaken identity, one of the absolute lads had said "Is that true, Ads? You don't know him?" and then the one called Adam had said "bleurgh" because he was too sloshed to respond. So as to why they had come to him and slammed a vodka jelly on his gentlemanly pub table in a nice old pub called the Engine and Tender, Mister Bob couldn't rightly say. It must have been some sort of internal bachelor recognition tendency, though where that had been on previous occasions when he'd really needed friendship Mister Bob didn't know.

Mister Bob relaxed into the cooling bathwater. He wondered briefly if his boiler back in Portobello had been fixed yet.

Happy old Portobello. Home of his books and his bathtime things. Except for his toothbrush and the GODDESS soap, that was. Those were in a paper bag somewhere in Dundee.

Mister Bob reached for the hotel soap. It was a horrible white block.

But it had once been the only sort of soap he'd ever used. He felt glad of his recent experiments, glad that there was a seemingly inexhaustible supply of luxury soap made from natural ingredients out there in the world, and glad that despite the hangover and his night of sweaty male-dominated insanity, his stink had not returned.

Mister Bob might have smelled a little gamey before he'd sunk into this bathtub but he had not, he knew, reeked of root vegetables.

A hot rock of magnetic pain marbled through his brain.

"Gah!" said Mister Bob.

He wondered if the pain would have been a Panic Vision if he had been the same person he was a few weeks ago. He wondered if the hangover had blocked the Vision (he had, after all, become addicted to booze in the first place because it presented a temporary escape from such things) or if he had been, thanks to the bathtimes of recent weeks, cured. It wasn't the time to know.

Mister Bob soaped his armpits and his inner thighs and, in the absence of shampoo, he soaped his head. He then threw the soap hopelessly in the direction of his feet as if a loosely-targeted lob might magically clean them too.

★

Mister Bob burped and the taste of battery acid came up into his mouth.

And then he threw up.

Hunks of stomach lining and what looked like Doner Kebab floated on the surface of the soap-greyed bathwater.

In his ceramic bowl of soup, in a hotel he couldn't remember the name of, in a town far removed from his life, Mister Bob suddenly felt very alone.

For a moment, in his post-puke euphoria, he found himself simply *being*.

So it *was* possible after all.

Parts of the night began to come back to him as he lay in the tub of increasingly cold water and bits of sick.

To start with, he could remember Desperate Dan. Dundee! He was in Dundee. Yes, he remembered Desperate Dan and how happy he'd been to see him.

Desperate Dan, of course, was a comic book hero Mister Bob remembered from childhood. Dundee was the town in which Dan and his other *Beano* and *Dandy* pals had come to life. Well, they came to life in Beanotown or, in the case of Dan, Cactusville USA, but they had been invented here. And to commemorate their being invented here, the people of Dundee or their council or something had erected a statue of Desperate Dan in the main High Street.

In his drunken slumber after the pubs had all closed and twelve or thirteen vodka jellies had been forced into his shuddering body, he had been very happy to see Desperate Dan.

He'd felt the precise emotions a person should feel when seeing a long-missed old friend.

In fact, he'd felt similar emotions when he'd been reunited with Mister Matey in a London Superdrug. About Matey, he'd been slightly bewildered as to how he could have forgotten about him and about Desperate Dan he'd felt an additional twinge of guilt as he recalled "growing out of him." He'd decided to stop reading those comics around the age of nine or ten because he'd wanted to grow up. He'd pushed Dan away and here, in the Dundee night, he could finally apologise.

"I'm sorry, Dan," Mister Bob had said on seeing the stubbly face of the world's strongest cowboy, "I'm so, so, sorry."

The stags had found him cuddling Dan's rain-wetted legs, said "you're fuckin' mental pal," and legged it.

Mister Bob had then puked on Dan's shoes.

Mister Bob was roused by a semi-familiar sound.

It was the sound of a key in a lock.

"Ooh, God, Housekeeping, sorry," said the cleaner and began to back out.

The hotel room turned out to be (for he had no

recollection of having previously seen the room in which he'd emerged from his stupor and semi-automatically drawn a hot bath) a studio-like affair with a bathtub and a bed essentially in the same room but with a plastic screen dividing the room into two relatively-, but not entirely convincingly-, distinct spaces.

"No, I know, it's okay," said Mister Bob, "please come back. Actually, I think I might need your help with something."

"What do you mean?" said Housekeeping, coming partially back into the room, "I'm not helping you with *that*."

Mister Bob realised he could have chosen his words more intelligently for a naked man in a bathtub with a saturated flannel on his head.

Housekeeping had probably seen far worse sights than this, but then she probably hadn't noticed the puke on the surface of the water yet. Though she clearly wanted to set limits on the sort of help she was willing to provide, she didn't seem particularly fazed by the sight of a naked Oliver Hardy lookalike going increasingly goose pimply in a bathtub.

She probably had to throw people out all the time. He could relate to this. Semi-regularly, he'd escorted drug addicts or homeless people or drunks from the toilets of trains. There was not usually much choice in such matters. Hoping they would leave of their own accord was too little and summoning the British Transport Police was too much.

"No, it's just that..." stammered Mister Bob, "I just

wonder if you can see any, ah, um, clothes out there, ah, um, in my room?"

The twin nuisances of "ah" and "um" had returned apparently.

"Clothes, is it?" said Housekeeping.

"Yes, I, ah," stuttered Mister Bob, "don't remember where I, um, put them."

There were shuffling, shambling noises as Housekeeping moved around on the other side of the plastic screen. Mister Bob patiently watched the condensation on the screen transforming gleefully back into water and running in rivulets down towards the orangey tartan linoleum. He shivered in a draft coming from goodness knew where. What kind of hotel was this? It was terrible. Just so ugly. It was as if the lowest possible standard of quality had been bobbed for by the people who had set the place up. In the 1970s, probably. Mister Bob had made the reservation himself but he couldn't remember anything about it. His inept phone screen-jabbing journey though hotels.com could have been an aeon ago.

"No-o!" said Housekeeping in a strangely positive almost sing-song way considering the bad news she was laying on him, "no clothes in 'ere."

"Ah," said Mister Bob, "in that case, we have a bit of a problem. That is, I, um, have a bit of a..."

"You want me to 'ave a look in lost property for you?" asked Housekeeping, surprisingly helpfully.

"Would you?"

"Right," said Housekeeping, "just a tick."

And then she was gone.

Mister Bob noticed that she had also left the door open behind her. From his position in the bathtub, he could see the linoleum of the hallway and the shiny number 18 on the door of the room opposite his. He shuddered and felt abruptly vulnerable.

Mister Bob sank back down into the bathtub, allowing the foetid water to cover his shoulders.

He sank further still, up to his nostrils, and indulged in some hippo-like snorting on the surface of the water. He felt like one of those coffee machines that steams the milk. He'd seen the baristas doing that in cafes, just chasing the milk around on the surface of the jug.

Small chunks of sick and carrot-coloured stomach lining floated on the surface, directly in Mister Bob's eyeline. It made the word "plumb-bob" appear in his mind though he couldn't place quite what such a thing was. The pointless thought reminded him of his time in his bathtub at home, the relaxing practice of non-judgmentally watching his rubbishy thoughts come and go without his conscious say-so. The reminder was welcome and it distracted him from the breeze coming from the open door and from his broader predicament.

The hotel had gone remarkably quiet. He could no longer hear Housekeeping shuffling around. One would expect a background of hotel noises; some purposeful bellhop back-and-forth perhaps or the tinny clatter of silverware and plates from the kitchen, regional accents saying "no, I ain't sin none since Wednesday" and "right you are then," as staff went about their hotellish business. But there was nothing.

The thought occurred to Mister Bob that he didn't know what time it was. *Shit.*

Mister Bob sat upright again.

He was supposed to be at Waverley tonight, which meant he had to be at Inverness this afternoon.

Maybe it already was this afternoon.

Somewhere, a seagull cackled.

For a naked man in a bucket of vomit without any clothes or even so much as a towel within reaching distance, Mister Bob felt remarkably calm. It was the hangover, of course. Nothing seemed particularly urgent during a hangover of this magnitude.

He wondered if he should or shouldn't pull the plug and let the water out. On the one hand, he'd been lucky that the cleaning lady hadn't noticed the chunks of sick and he now had a chance to keep it that way by draining the water and using his hands to scoop the chunks out of the drain trap, dignity preserved. On the other, he would be completely exposed to the non-watery elements, naked before the world , if he did. He decided to stay where he was, obscured by the bathwater.

Mister Bob sank down again in the water and rippled at the meniscus with his nostrils.

He rolled his eyes towards his feet and wiggled his toes, the water making the slightly echoing *splishy-splishy* noises indigenous to bathtubs.

It crossed his mind insanely that perhaps there was only one world bathtub. That, when you're in the bath, you're connected to everyone else who happens to be in a bathtub at that moment. The bathtub in which you currently wallow, Mister Bob mused, might only be an outpost of a far greater infrastructure of bathtubs. The drain, after all, was a fairly direct connection with the ocean. And there was, after all, only "one water" in the world, albeit one temporarily fractured into dispersed islands of oceans and seas and rivers and lakes and water tanks and bathtubs and hot water bottles and snowglobes. It was silly to think that the water of the world wasn't aware of its separateness and the inevitability of its reunion with itself. Silly. Silly is what that would be.

Despite the connections between all filled and partially-filled bathtubs, you probably couldn't communicate with someone else in their bathtub on the other side of the world.

Not unless you really concentrated.

Mister Bob rose from the water like Godzilla, the smelly water dripping from his chin and earlobes and nipples and cheekbones and collarbone.

"Ah," he said, "um, hello?"

There was nothing. He could faintly hear the rumble of distant traffic, the sort of noise a person usually tunes out. It gave him hope that maybe it was still morning after all, that the traffic noise was the noise of whatever passed for a Dundee rush hour. Those comic books wouldn't draw themselves.

Biff! Boff! Thunk. Arooo!

Those were the sounds made by the Bash Street Kids and Dennis the Menace and Gnasher in the comics. Mister Bob remembered Gnasher, Dennis' big-toothed spider-furred dog who could gnash his way even through concrete and liked to chase postmen. It was horrible really. Like something from a nightmare.

Gnasher, lest we forget, also enjoyed tearing the seats out of fat men's trousers, revealing polka dot underpants beneath. Fat men in those comics usually had highly inventive names like "Fatty Fudge, portly buffoon" and spent most of their time eating chains of sausages and vast mountains of mashed potato and bending over to pick up a dropped sweetie only to reveal their arses to Dennis's catapult or Gnasher's tungsten teeth.

Was this fattist violence what passed for comedy in Dundee? Well, it did today, Mister Bob supposed. He did indeed feel like a portly buffoon.

"Right," said Housekeeping, returning from the hallway. Mister Bob hadn't heard her coming up the stairs or along the landing or anything. She had been silent. A wraith. Even so, the relief inspired in Mister Bob by her reappearance was palpable. What if she'd forgotten all about him or she'd fallen down the stairs or had suffered a stroke and died or the world had ended like in *Day of the Triffids* leaving him stranded in his sick-soupy tub with no clothes and no ally? But none of this had happened. She had returned. Everything was going to be fine.

The woman who had introduced herself to Mister Bob as Housekeeping unfolded an extra large t-shirt. It had a picture of Homer Simpson looking unwell on it. Under her arm was tucked a pair of dumb guy bluejeans.

"Are these yours?" she asked. "They were the only things I could see in there."

Mister Bob ogled the hopeless threads in dismay.

"Yes," said Mister Bob.

Dried and dressed and afforded half an hour of privacy by the cleaning lady, Mister Bob was relieved to find his wallet and mobile phone wedged inside one of his shoes at the foot of the bed.

Luckier still, his other shoe was present too, albeit sitting improbably on the toilet cistern. So happy was he to be given these rays of hope in his time of absolute crisis, Mister Bob kissed his own shoe.

He looked at himself in the mirror. He looked awful, like some horrible ornament on the tartan linoleum. There were bags under his eyes and his wet thinning hair hung forward limply. He would now have to make the walk of shame from the hotel, along the high street, and down Crichton Street where all the shoppers and commuters and tourists and intercity art twats getting off the train to see the new V&A would marvel at his horrible costume.

And then, of course, to work. He would keep an eye out for a shop somewhere along the way for a change of clothes.

Oh, why had he gotten so drunk? His head was beginning to pulse.

Thrub, thrub, thrub.

★

Mister Bob passed an unstaffed reception desk on his way out of the hotel. He looked around for someone to say goodbye to and to thank for the terrible clothes (terrible was right but it was better than the alternative) but all he saw was a visitor book splayed open with a bic biro pen.

Mister Bob anonymously signed and dated the book and when confronted with a COMMENTS column , instead of writing something like "thank you for understanding" or "thanks for the pants," he wrote, immaturely, "Bob fancies Tracey." After everything, he was still enjoying the freedom of an alien town.

"Bob fancies Tracey" was there forever now. He had inscribed their names in the Tablet of Eternity. They were as good as married really.

Seven

"Welcome on board this *frrvrrfrrr* service," said the automated welcome message on the train, "to *frrvrrfrrr* and *frrvrrfrrr*, calling at *frrvrrfrrr*, *frrvrrfrrr*, and *frrvrrfrrr*."

Well done, thought Mister Bob. It was only the important information that you managed to obfuscate with static while every bit of phatic drivel came through crystal clear. Singularly perfect. If the railway company had been asked to do that, he was not sure they'd have been capable of it. It was lightning in a bottle.

Moreover, the "welcome on board" part of the message rubbed him up the wrong way somehow. Shouldn't it be "welcome *a*board?" He hoped they hadn't paid someone to write this shit.

He'd noticed before that these announcements and various signs that had appeared around the railway network in the past few years referred to "customers" instead of "passengers." While not, strictly speaking, untrue, it still betrayed a certain managerial and private-sector mentality that indicated to Mister Bob (a) bad tidings for the way he would be treated at work and (b) the end of the world. It was a minor eschatological detail that few people but Mister Bob would notice. It was a combination of his familiarity with the granular nuances of the English language and his unnatural capacity for imagining doom.

A pretty trans girl with an up-high ponytail and a polyester railway company uniform, a colleague he recognised but did not know, marched down the aisle with a mobile phone pressed snugly to her ear. The railway company did not issue mobile phones to its team members so it must have been her personal phone. Mister Bob recognised the frustration of having to fall back on your personal assets to solve problems at work. It crossed a line. "There were no hot snacks for me at Preston," the colleague was saying, "I've been to Edinburgh and back with no snacks. I can't do nothing now can I?... What?... How can I give you the reference number for a delivery I didn't receive?"

Central Operations being as helpful as ever, thought Mister Bob, as the ponytail flicked through the sliding doors at the end of the coach.

An obnoxious family on a day out began to sing

further down the coach. "Row-row-row your boat, gently down the streeeeam! If you see a crocodile, don't forget to scream, *YAAAARGH!*"

Good *God*, they actually screamed. On public transport. What a bunch of bastards.

The peace of yesterday's easygoing morning, of noticing the golden gleam of the morning light on his house key as he'd locked the door at the start of this journey, had been destroyed by twelve vodka jellies forced onto him by a platoon of revelling lads. Had it not been his intention to get blotto though? Yes, it had been. He could not blame the lads. Then again, perhaps the chaos had really begun with the mystery of the spunking cock he'd found in his jacket pocket. Ever since he found it, had there not been a sense of upside-downness? Since he found that spunking cock, everything had been out of control. *He* had been out of his own control, peaceful morning or otherwise.

When did I lose my freedom, thought Mister Bob as he watched the Lowlands fly by outside the window, *when did I lose my ability to choose?*

Mister Bob had not exactly chosen the events of the night before. They'd just happened. Despite his chaos feelings, these events even as they were happening had a certain inevitably. It was something more like Sod's Law than Fatalism. Talking to Pavel, travelling to Waverley, working the trolley service. It was as if all events running up to the present moment had made it inevitable, which, Mister Bob now supposed, was true.

God, he felt terrible. The light from the windows hurt his eyes. The motion of the train made him feel sick. The singing cheerfulness of the family on their day out made his head throb and his soul feel ever more at odds with where it, perhaps, should be. Should his soul be elsewhere? Or was it right where it was supposed to be?

When he was a child, before everything felt inevitable or preordained, he assumed he would grow up to become something worthwhile and, at the very least, to get married to someone relatively pleasant and to raise his own family. Had that been the idle fantasy of a juvenile mind or was it, in fact, where he was supposed to be now and he'd taken a wrong turn somewhere along the way?

These questions weren't making Mister Bob feel any better. He staggered off to the bathroom, slightly hunched. The hunch was a reflex: if he was going to throw up, he would want it to hit the floor in the least splattery way, so the hunch reduced the distance his chunks would have to fall. Mister Bob realised he had been in positions like this one too many times in his life. It was a good job he was Getting Better.

Mister Bob made his way along the corridor to the toilet where he pressed the big round < > button only for nothing to happen. The button flashed red to indicate that the toilet was occupied. Mister Bob wasn't sure he would make it the full length of another carriage to another vestibule toilet. It wasn't worth the risk of struggling through the carriage, being taken short, and vomiting on someone's head.

He wondered which sort of passenger head would be the worst sort of passenger head to barf all over. He would be very embarrassed to cover a sweet old woman's head with sick, he knew that much. Or if it was a young teenage girl and all of her friends started "freaking out" and screaming, there would be a lot of trouble for him. He could picture the girl now, wiping the stomach acid from her eyes and saying "ew, no."

A tough guy would be a bad person to chuck on too. He'd silently stand, his leather biker's jacket covered in Heinz vegetable soup, coming to his full size, and ram his fist so far down Mister Bob's throat, he'd be able to make his anus speak like a glove puppet.

An overly confident business person would be a good person to be sick on. Mister Bob didn't want to be sick on anyone but, if he had to, that would be his first choice. A business person with a bluetooth earpiece with someone on the other end of the line saying "Greg, Greg, I'm not hearing you very well, Greg. What about the quarterly turnover figures? Greg? Are you going through a tunnel?"

Yes, thought Mister Bob, *that would be fine actually*.

The singing family on their day out would be a shame to throw up on. Being sick all over the dad's head could be funny though and would give the kids something to talk about for years to come. Maybe he could vomit violently over their Travel Monopoly board, sending the little houses and hotels flying. "Oh *really!*" the dad would say, "I must insist on speaking to the train manager!" the dad would say. And the boy kid would say "Haha, do *not* pass go, daddy, do *not* collect two hundred pounds!" And the girl kid would start crying.

On reflection, the worst head to be sick on would be the head of a baby in a pushchair. If nobody noticed that he'd been sick into the pushchair, he could probably walk away from it. That would protect his dignity somewhat but he'd always wonder how things played out afterwards, when someone came along and saw the baby's head all covered in sick.

Was this all a Panic Vision? No, not quite. But Mister Bob still felt faintly depressed by it.

The person in the toilet was not coming out. Mister Bob couldn't hear any motion inside the giant Coca-Cola can that served as a railway company bathroom. He was getting desperate.

Mister Bob banged on the door.

He suddenly had the Vision—a real old-fashioned Panic Vision, so bad was his stress level now—of the door rumbling open to reveal an old lady on the toilet and, the smell of her shit reaching Mister Bob's nostrils causing him to projectile vomit into the tiny room and over her tasselled loafers.

Returning to reality, Mister Bob was glad in a way that door had not opened when he'd banged it.

He looked at the red-lit < > symbol and panicked slightly. He didn't know what to do.

His gorge rose.

He could no longer contain himself. The sick rushed up his oesophagus and onwards to freedom.

Mister Bob's vomit ran heftily down the bathroom door. The chunks hit the floor on the metallic connection point between the vestibule carpet and the vinyl he knew to be inside the cubicle. The liquid content of his puke slid down the surface of the door more slowly than the chunks had done.

Mister Bob knew what to do next. He ruefully staggered over to the intercom and pressed the button. "Aye?" said an affronted Tyneside voice through the intercom. The voice, Mister Bob knew, originated in the buffet cart. Mister Bob could hear the cappuccino machine in the background.

"Ah," said Mister Bob, "Yes, hello, this is Bob Forrester, I'm a railway company employee and a passenger on this train." He stopped briefly to take a breath. "Someone has made a mess, um, been sick I'm afraid, in the vestibule of Coach G. I thought you'd like to know."

"Oh aye, greet," said the tinny Geordie, pausing to sigh, "Ee, thanks mate, I'll send someone doon."

Mister Bob hid in Coach F, the quiet carriage. There were signs on the walls of this carriage asking passengers ("customers," actually) to keep conversation to a minimum and to silence their phones. Mister Bob approved of such measures. He hunkered down and tried to rest.

Two elderly team members had decided to use the coach for their twenty-minute tea break in the seats directly behind Mister Bob's.

"This one's the whole family," said one of the women.

"Ooh," said the other, "who's the little funny one at the end?"

"That's Marvin," said the first woman, "he's got Down's Syndrome."

"Ooh," said the other, "and how about this little lad, has he got Down's as well?"

"That's my dad's wife," said the first woman, "she's Chinese."

Mister Bob knew that, physically speaking, he could stand up and find another seat. He was not, however, *spiritually* free to do so. He could not risk them seeing him leave lest they snigger at him for being aloof. They would make a limp-wristed gesture behind his back and say "ooooh" and Mister Bob would die.

"Ooh, Chinese?" said the second woman, "Did they meet over there?"

"Noooooo, they met in the pub."

And on and on.

Mister Bob wished he could insulate himself from the madness.

Mister Bob wished he could pull the black velvet hood of night over his head.

"We all have trouble at home, don't we?" said one of the team members with a tone of working-class solidarity, if not conspiracy, "But we can come into work for a natter."

★

Just two short hours after befouling a vestibule, Mister Bob arrived at the Sleeper departure platform at Inverness. He tried to affect an aura of professional pulledtogetherness. He felt like a revolting slug.

Mister Bob felt firecrackers in his temples and he could tell that his tongue was coated with a thin film of yellowish slime. Visualising it, Mister Bob supposed it must look like the yellowed windows of the 124 bus and it gave him a shudder to think there could be any connection, even just a symbolic one, between those windows and his tongue.

There was a plaque on the wall of the railway station and Mister Bob looked at it through crusted eyes. He wanted to look into a mirror to check the pallidness of his reflection, but there was no mirror around so the evolutionary vestige within him that demanded a mirror (and also to avoid the gaze of judgemental passersby) would have to be satisfied with this performative examination of a meaningless plaque. The plaque read:

THIS RAILWAY EXTENDED FROM
THE TOWN OF NAIRN TO KEITH
COMPLETING THE COMMUNICATION
BETWEEN LONDON AND INVERNESS

Yes, thought Mister Bob, thank goodness for that. Had that "communication" not been completed, there would have been no sleeper train and no need for sleeper attendants such as himself and he would not be standing here now, rattlesnakes squirming in his gut.

Mister Bob felt cast asunder on the torrents of history. The construction of the line between London and Inverness had nothing to do with him, it all taking place over a century before his birth. Events were put in motion long before The Invention of Mister Bob. Mister Bob had just fallen into them.

WAS BEGUN IN OCT 1856 AND OPENED FOR PUBLIC TRAFFIC ON 18 AUGUST 1858

Just twenty months to build a whole railway station. The past sure was tense. He supposed it had been important to get it all set up as quickly as possible to ensure an indentured future for millions of wage slaves yet to be born. There was an idea that coal was the fuel of Empire but its real fuel was the population of the future, the promise of Soylent Green Forever.

The very top of the plaque showed a heraldic unicorn, a mounted knight, and the Hand of God protruding from a cloud. The Hand grasped a wreath and seemed to be flexing its bicep.

It struck Mister Bob as amusing that anyone should think God would be involved one way or another in the construction of a railway line, but why not? If God was involved in the affairs of human beings at all, was it any more absurd that He be involved in a railway extension? God was the god of railway engineers, just as He was the god of boa constrictors, grandfather clocks, false teeth and bathtime. Well, that bathtime should be overseen by God almost went without saying. Cleanliness, after all, was next to It. Today, Mister Bob felt cut loose from God.

The plaque also showed two young chaps, each of them naked but for a little pair of pants made from laurel leaves.

Having gleaned approximately nothing, Mister Bob roundly slugged his way to the station master's office to collect his stupid clipboard.

Mister Bob squinted into the eyes of the furious ham-faced Englishman. What was his problem? Maybe he always looked furious. The man looked almost naturally irritated, as if even the slightest conversation with another person was a waste of his time or perhaps a waste of his money or some other asset Mister Bob had not the experience to imagine.

"And your name please, sir?" said Mister Bob.

"You have an English accent," said the Londoner.

"Well spotted, sir." said Mister Bob, electric shocks going off on either side of his eyeballs. It was all he could manage.

"Surprising," said the Londoner, "I'd have thought..."

"I've lived in Scotland all of my life, sir," said Mister Bob, "I do not say I am Scottish but..."

Some sick came up into the back of Mister Bob's mouth and he swallowed it down again. It tasted green.

"What is your name please, sir?" Mister Bob managed again.

"Hargreevs," said the Londoner, "Samuel Aitch Hargreeves."

Mister Bob found the name Hargreeves on the list attached to his clipboard. It was right where it was supposed to be. They could do wonderful things with computers nowadays. It was a wonder they couldn't use computers to check people in so that Mister Bob didn't need to stand here, ticking names off a list by hand, and being shouted at and interrogated when he was so sleepy and ill.

Mister Bob neatly crossed the name off the list.

"Thank you, sir," said Mister Bob, unsure of whether all this "sirring" would infuriate the Londoner or if dropping it would infuriate him all the more. It was hard to know.

"May I continue now?" asked Samuel Aitch Hargreeves, furious.

"Yes please, sir, if you could continue to Coach B, you'll find your berth ready and waiting."

The Londoner continued along the platform. Mister Bob watched him go, the taste of sick still acrid in his mouth. Samuel Aitch Hargreeves stopped irritably to read each digital display panel on each door, in pursuit of Coach B. Mister Bob knew he'd gone the wrong way, of course, and so, probably, did the man himself but it was too soon for him to make a u-turn and to pass Mister Bob again with any dignity. Better to summon more fury and pretend this was all someone else's fault. Perhaps the furious man was right in a way. If the "communication" between London and Inverness had not been completed in 1856, the poor fellow would not have been in this humiliating position.

"*Robert*," came another furious voice. This one, however, was less amusing and it put the fear into Mister Bob.

Mister Bob turned dopily into the bloodshot eyes of the manager himself. And he was pissed off. Sunny was always pissed off but this time it felt more serious than usual. His beard still looked lovely though and it smelled of sandalwood. Mister Bob, despite his compromised state and the evil taste in his mouth, also registered the landmine shrapnel scarring on Sunny's cheeks.

"Hello Sunny," said Mister Bob.

"Don't hello me, Robert," hissed the train manager, "what the hopping Swiss *fuck* are you wearing? Where is your uniform?"

Mister Bob's polyester railway company uniform was hanging from a flagpole outside the Dundee City Chambers.

That is, the jacket and shirt were hanging from the flagpole. The trousers were wrapped around the neck of a statue of Minnie the Minx, © D.C. Thomson & Co. Ltd., in the town centre.

Mister Bob was unsure whether Sunny wanted an honest answer or not.

"Ah," said Mister Bob for the first time in a while,

for he had been taken off-guard by this question and had in fact completely forgotten about the nature of his current attire and what had happened to his polyester railway company uniform until now, "I, um, forgot it."

"You forgot it?" Sunny repeated.

"Yes," said Mister Bob.

"Yes *what?*" spat Sunny.

This last question confused Mister Bob greatly. They didn't address each other as "sir" or "ma'am" or anything like that in the railway company.

"Ah," said Mister Bob, "Yes, um... Sunny?"

"I should think *so*," said Sunny, apparently sexually aroused by hearing his name spoken aloud by a balding middle-aged man who smelled of sick, "now go to the station manager's office immediately and change out of this... whatever this is."

Mister Bob looked down at his clothes. He was wearing an untucked white t-shirt with a stoned off-brand Homer Simpson on it. Oh dear.

"Yes, Sunny," said Mister Bob and began to leave.

"And before you leave," said Sunny, "a word to the wise. You need to sort yourself out, Robert. You need to start turning up to work on time, you need to learn how to present yourself professionally, and it couldn't hurt if you lost some fucking weight."

Mister Bob's head hurt too much for this barrage to hit him very directly. Even so, the train manager's Brummie accent seemed to be rotting in his ear holes and it made him feel sick.

"I do all of those things already, Sunny."

"I beg your pardon?"

"Well, aside from losing weight, that is. I'm happy with the way I look." This was not entirely true but those Tumblr women had had a profound effect on him. He wanted to be positive. "And when have I ever failed to show up on time? I was on time even today. And today is the first time I've ever failed to wear my uniform. I'm just... not very well is all."

"If you're not well," said Sunny, "you should have phoned in sick."

"The trouble is, Sunny," said Mister Bob, "it takes me hours, sometimes even a whole day, to get to work. If standing here and checking names off a list can be described as work, that is. Sometimes I feel perfectly fine when I leave the house and then, on the way, circumstances change."

"Circumstances change," said Sunny in a mocking sarcastic tone, "yes, well." Sunny clearly knew that Mister Bob had reported for work either drunk or hungover after a serious drink-a-thon. Sunny was not born yesterday after all. In fact, Sunny had been born in 1975.

"Just pull yourself together," said Sunny, and then, as if he thought the message had not yet hit home, "sort yourself out."

But... I'm Getting Better, thought Mister Bob wimpishly.

Sunny took the clipboard from Mister Bob, seemingly to take over the so-called job while Mister Bob went off to get changed. Mister Bob could feel Sunny resisting the violent urge to slap his arse with the clipboard as he turned away from him.

But then, Sunny slapped Mister Bob's arse with the clipboard anyway. "The fuckin' state of you," said Sunny.

Mister Bob paused while he weighed up the merits of taking issue with what, in reality, was an assault. But Mister Bob couldn't, in the disorientation of the moment, see how an objection could be worth the fuss. Instead, he continued in his sleepy drift to the station master's office.

People talked about work as if it was something they did by choice, like it was a game to have fun with, when really it was a nightmare of enforced servitude. It wasn't slavery apparently because you were paid for it and had "chosen" to do it, had even competed with others to do it through application forms and interviews, but when you had no choice but to earn money to pay for your meagre rental flat life or face destitution could it really be said to be a choice? Was it so different to being violently forced into an addictive drug and then into sex work to pay for your habit? It was worse in a way, thought Mister Bob, since all you wanted were the elemental basics of dignity. Why wasn't it an inalienable human right to access a modest roof and some food and a few books to read? What was the point of civilisation if those things couldn't be guaranteed without being coerced into servitude?

What agency was there? What respite? All you could do was catch a moment here and a moment there, stolen in store cupboards and employee bathrooms (or in Mister Bob's case, sleeper train bunk berths and passenger toilets with unreliable doors) and to try against all reasonable hope to maintain a sense of self.

You weren't really free when you were at home, reading a book or having a bath or sitting on the toilet.

It seemed to Mister Bob that when a person wasn't actually working they were getting ready for work or recovering from work. You were only paid for the time you spent working, not for the other two thirds of the day even if they were lived in service to work. Those were the three modalities. The three flavours of wage slavery.

Stifling a yawn as he slotted the key card into the door of his sleeping cabin at midnight, Mister Bob once again wore his polyester railway company uniform. Well, he wore an approximation of it at least. A line of wall-mounted pegs in the station master's office at Waverley was home to a variety of mismatched uniform parts left behind by escaped railway company employees. The purpose of this contractual stipulation was for the railway company to scrape back something they'd invested in those employees by insisting that they leave their uniforms uselessly behind when moving on to pastures new. The result was a cache of useless uniforms of various shapes and sizes, an asset apparently, but more like a line of sloughed skins. Mister Bob had once seen David McManaman wipe his teaspoon on the cuff of a polyester sleeve after making his mid-morning tea.

For better or worse, "pastures new" for railway company employees usually meant retirement. Thanks to an admittedly half-decent pension scheme—a vestige from the days of public ownership—most railway workers held onto their jobs to the bitter end. There were, after all, far worse and less secure jobs out there. Mister Bob had weighed the alternatives many times in his imagination and no matter how he squinted sideways at the vision, he just couldn't see himself as a Deliveroo driver.

He switched on the lights of the sleeping cabin and put his wallet and phone down on the tiny tabletop by the miniature wash basin.

Mister Bob knew about the mishmash of abandoned uniforms in the station master's office but had never imagined that he'd end up wearing one of them. He usually kept his own polyester duds in excellent condition and looked forward to a day when he could travel between Glasgow and Edinburgh benders on his pensioner's rail pass and scan the the vista for his permanently vacated uniform now adorning its proud new owner: a scarecrow in a field.

What a day. All of Mister Bob's days, when working, were long. But this day had been long and a real stinker.

There was a rat-a-tat-tat at the door. It sounded impish. What now?

Polyester tie already half off, Mister Bob opened the door, expecting the worst. Surely some toilet was blocked or some overly-entitled passenger needed an additional box of Monarch of the Glen soaps or somesuch.

It was Tracey!

"Hello Tracey," said Mister Bob in genuine surprise, "I didn't know you were working tonight."

"I am," she said more earnestly than she normally spoke, "well, I was supposed to get off at Preston with the hot snacks but I decided to stay on for an extra half-shift. Listen Bob, I saw what happened at Waverley. Sunny had no right to speak to you like that. It was more than the usual crap. He's such a wanker."

Mister Bob was almost speechless. He almost couldn't believe there had been a witness. His feelings hung in a state between validation, that someone knew that Sunny had shouted at him and slapped his arse with a clipboard, and shame that someone had witnessed Sunny shouting at him and slapping his arse with a clipboard. All while he'd been standing in a Homer Simpson knock-off t-shirt, eyes still glassy from his ill-remembered adventures in vodka jelly.

"You saw that," said Mister Bob redundantly.

"Yeah," said Tracey, spinning coquettishly back and forth on her heels and reaching out to take his paw in her claw, "it was bullshit."

Tracey was holding his hand and he did not

withdraw it. Her skin had a natural coolness like the hands of a pastry chef.

Tracey kissed Mister Bob's cheek tenderly. His heart beat heavy in his chest. An internal security camera scanned the inside of his head rapidly to make sure that this wasn't a Panic Vision. It wasn't. This was actually happening.

He felt a surge of excitement rise in his chest, one floor up from the sensation of the butterflies of excitement he'd not experienced for so long and had long judged missing-presumed-dead. And a twitch came from inside his borrowed pants.

"Look," said Tracey, "I haven't got much time. The boss is still on the war path and I've got a load of shitters to clean."

It wasn't exactly the romantic moment one usually saw in films.

Tracey got down on her knees and unfastened the plastic top button of her polyester railway company shirt. "Come on then," she said hurriedly, her original accent suddenly hitting hard, "Gonna gie me a gobba Bob?"

Mister Bob practically couldn't believe this was happening. But it was. He was certain this was no Panic Vision. This was really real. It was too bad that he was in such a state with his hangover, that Tracey would not get to enjoy the full benefits of SNOW FAIRY and GODDESS and Mister Matey. He wanted her to know that he'd taken her suggestion to heart. Next time perhaps? But that was getting ahead of himself insanely. This was, miraculously, happening now.

There was something about Tracey's gestures that struck Mister Bob as matter-of-fact but not overly practised. He could see Tracey as a teenager striking the same pose in the quiet part of some municipal car park at night for a boyfriend, but there was something that told him she hadn't done this for a while. A creak to the knee perhaps.

He touched the zipper of his borrowed polyester railway company trousers with the tip of his thumb, only for:

RATTA-TAT-TAT, came the knock at the door, this time with an accent of impatience and more than a tinge of anger. Only one person on the train would knock like that.

Mister Bob briefly considered ignoring it but Sunny would only use his train manager's key card to override the lock and then it would all be over.

Tracey quickly got up from the cabin floor and dived into the lower bunk, bringing her knees up to her chest, in the same position behind the door she had taken the last time she and Mister Bob were alone in a similar cabin together.

Mister Bob opened the cupboard-like door of the cabin to reveal the all-too-predictable face of the train manager. Predictably, Sunny looked pissed off, and Mister Bob was concerned that he was looking for Tracey, perhaps to complete some horrible chore of cleaning up the puke of a motion-sick passenger, and that Sunny knew somehow that she was here.

Mister Bob saw the righteous fury in the train manager's eyes and what Mister Bob unimaginatively now saw were chickenpox scars on his cheeks.

As Mister Bob opened his parched end-of-day mouth to say something he hoped would sound professional (though he wasn't sure what could possibly come out), Sunny spoke first. "And another thing," said Sunny, as if the conversation on the railway station concourse hours previously had not been abruptly terminated with a surprising but definite (and, Mister Bob now knew, witnessed) physical assault, "I've filed a report with Base Command about your antics today. You'll be hearing something from them soon."

Sunny stormed off passionately down the corridor and away before Mister Bob could hear the stifled tittering of his friend behind the door.

Mister Bob closed the door firmly and Tracey fell about. She was rolling around in a hedgehog ball at the foot of his bunk, cackling like a devil.

"Base Command!" she mocked.

"Yes," said Mister Bob, "Fucking hell."

Only those who had drunk deep of the corporate Kool Aid would ever use such a phrase. "Base Command" was where the head honchos gathered to push bullshit around meeting rooms, dung beetle-like, in an office building near Calton Hill. It used to be called HQ and before that it had been called The Railway Building. For some reason, the private-sector corporation who had taken over everything just after the turn of the millennium, enjoyed a military-like terminology in their daily work but nobody beyond that caste of twats ever actually used it. Except for Sunny it seemed. He had betrayed the secret that he had his bloodshot eye on the corporate ladder.

"And filed a report!" said Tracey.

"Sent a text message more like," said Mister Bob, "what a, ah, um.. What a... wanker."

Mister Bob got into the bunk in front of Tracey in a mirror image of how they had last sat together on a bunk while gliding through the lowlands at forty miles per hour. It was the usual face-to-face position in which Mister Bob thought of Tracey whenever he thought of Tracey (which he did *a lot*) since that birthday night. Though his back was to the window, Mister Bob knew that the giant shadows of giant windmills made their giant stride through the night.

There were no cans of premium strength lager this time, so Mister Bob pulled an old-fashioned hip flask from his capacious trouser pockets and tossed it in Tracey's direction.

"Good lad," she said with a sense of admiration as she caught it.

"Nice catch," said Mister Bob uselessly. The flask had only been in the air for half a second.

Tracey unscrewed the cap and took a swig. "Urgh," she said, "What is it?"

"No idea," said Mister Bob, "I borrowed these trousers from the office. That flask was in the pocket."

Tracey threw the flask back at him, laughing, "oh, you dirty bastard!"

"It's okay," said Mister Bob, "it's not old. I think David McManaman probably stashed it in there," and he took a swig for himself. He recognised the drink as something called Glayva. He'd had David pegged as a whiskey man so the sickly-sweet tang came as a mild surprise. Maybe it hadn't been David's at all. Mister Bob wasn't particularly interested.

"Did you get my note then," said Tracey after a pause. Mister Bob noticed that the pause wasn't an awkward one. It was the first time he'd experienced a pause that wasn't awkward in years. He felt remarkably at ease here in the bunk with Tracey, comfortable in a way he didn't usually feel. Not beyond recent submergences in the bathtub anyway. He took a moment to appreciate how he didn't feel nagged by Panic Visions. A lingering embarrassment about the previous night was certainly enough to prompt one.

The previous night. It was only the previous night so far as the calendar was concerned. Mister Bob hadn't slept properly in about thirty hours. His internal clock told him that "last night" was part of one monster day of tedious work and bleak escapist leisure.

"Your note?" said Mister Bob.

"I put it in your jacket pocket when Death Breath was at the door. Last time, I mean."

So it *had* been Tracey. Well, of course. Who else?

"Oh, *that*," said Mister Bob, "I did." And he laughed, which started Tracey off again. She was biting one of her fingernails charmingly and he passed her the flask again. "Ah, cheeky, um, cheeky monkey," he said.

"Come on then," said Tracey, "let's have it out."

Mister Bob unfastened the button of his borrowed polyester railway company uniform trousers and unzipped the fly. He pulled down the front of his underpants, last seen slumped on the linoleum floor of a Dundee hotel room, and let his erection unfold into the room. He noticed a trail of pre-cum on the inside of his underpants from his previous arousal, from before they'd been interrupted by the knock at the door. It didn't even occur to Mister Bob to try not to think of Sunny's scornful expression or anything else that could risk his erection; he was happy and comfortable and he was glad to be, ah, um, *out*.

"Choo-Choo!" said Tracey somewhat inexplicably, while making the gesture of a long-distance trucker pulling the horn. She tossed the flask back in Miser Bob's direction and it landed on the bunk's soft albeit economically thin mattress.

Mister Bob laughed and unscrewed the flask cap, penis bobbing gamely in Tracey's direction, and took a sip. As he did so, Tracey pulled her shoes off and tugged off her socks, dropping each component carelessly over the side and onto the floor. He wasn't quite sure what she had in mind.

Tracey snuggled down a little and extended her legs. She gently cupped her feet around Mister Bob's penis and massaged it up and down. The soles of her feet had the same pastry chef coolness he'd noticed on her hands earlier. Their skin was slightly coarse, a souvenir of thirty years spent walking up and down train aisles and corridors, but softened by the disciplined application of Nivea cream, which Mister Bob fancied he could now smell lightly in the air.

As Mister Bob and Tracey footjobbed their way along the spine of the Pennines and while Sunny stormed his way up and down the corridors, cursing and muttering and making careerist promises that would show them all, the giants outside the window marched steadily and silently through the peaceful night.

Mister Bob weebled unsteadily into the narrow hallway of the Caledonian Sleeper. To maximise bunk space, people being able to sleep through a night journey being the whole point of these trains, the 'Sleeper had been designed and built with exceptionally narrow corridors. Not for the first time, the irony occurred to Mister Bob that such a large man should have landed a job involving such tight squeezes. He was uniquely ill-qualified for it.

The thought crossed his mind only briefly, however. Mister Bob was feeling far too proud of himself, far too happy at the occurrence that Chance had placed in his path, so fully cheered by the change in his circumstances, that he wasn't particularly interested in the way his workplace had been designed around what a Tumblr person might call The Thin

Ideal. He was far too happy to dwell on such trivialities. In fact, he wondered why it had entered his head at all.

It was, of course, state memory striking again. He was in the train corridor, having train corridor thoughts.

Just as soapy bathtime bliss would provide a mental "state" that connected Mister Bob to bathtimes of yesteryear and perhaps also those yet to come, this narrow train corridor provided a "state" in which Mister Bob would normally have bland thoughts about its narrowness. He had been prompted, triggered, to have a particular kind of thought by this particular environment. What hope, Mister Bob wondered, for free will among humans if all we do is blunder along between different environmentally triggered mindstates? Free will. What a joke. Mister Bob had enjoyed remarkably little free will in his life. He was evidence against the hypothesis that such a thing could exist. He had not intended to become a balding, moustachioed singleton. It had happened to him, he knew, because states had happened to him. He had blundered through the wrong states again and again. But if one could choose which states one blundered through, could perhaps something approximating free will be arrived at? It was, Mister Bob felt, an interesting and important question.

But first, a poo.

Just as his Panic Visions only ever lasted for a fraction of a second, this line of thought about narrow corridors and life's little ironies and free will being either a bleak joke or else eminently achievable once one cracked the mystery of how to navigate between different environmental states, lasted barely a moment. His thought process was back onto his poo and also his astonishing moment of good luck. A good thing had happened to Mister Bob and he wanted to take a moment to recognise it as such.

Yes, A Good Thing had happened for once to Mister Bob.

As Mister Bob progressed along the corridor, his sides brushed along the walls of the corridor. The polyester sleeves of his borrowed polyester railway company uniform made a swiffing noise as they rubbed along the bulkheads. He *swiffed* down the corridor, the polyester sleeves catching briefly on the external part of each berth's door locking mechanism, until he came to the toilet.

Mister Bob pressed the familiar door-opening button. It was the size of a large coin and displayed the strange < > symbol, which he had always supposed was intended to resemble a pair of opening doors. But the door of the toilet didn't look like that at all. The door to the toilet was, lest we forget, round.

Mister Bob had once read something about the symbols that were now being designed to communicate something along the lines of "turn back! extreme danger!" to anyone who should chance upon humanity's buried nuclear shame. The challenge was, apparently, to convey this meaning to any future humans or newly-evolved species or unfortunate alien visitors, none of whom could be assumed to be able to read English or any other current language or indeed language at all. The new symbols had to convey a vitally important message under circumstances that were very hard to imagine in advance. Countless anthropologists, linguists, cultural experts, science-fiction writers, psychologists, and zoologists were working on it. Mister Bob was impressed that such efforts were being made. Humanity hadn't even designed a train toilet door to anyone's satisfaction yet. Or rather, they *had*, but then they'd overthought things as usual and replaced it with something ridiculous. Mister Bob wondered if the design process for the nuclear warning symbol had arrived at this level of advanced second-guessing yet. Mister Bob felt that it was best to keep things simple.

The toilet door rumbled open pathetically. A mild smell of chemicals and urine hit Mister Bob's nostrils. For the first time in Mister Bob's life or, more specifically, the first time since he'd become involved with soap bars called SNOW FAIRY and GODDESS, Mister Bob found himself offended by a smell.

Mister Bob noticed a small black square on the floor.

It was a wallet.

Mister Bob picked it up.

If this wallet contained a wad of cash, he wondered if he had the morality within himself to report it to the British Transport Police or to take it to lost property at Euston. Maybe, instead, he would take it back to his cabin and to Tracey, and show her what he had found.

He suspected Tracey would suggest they split the cash or else take it on an exciting night on the town. Mister Bob honestly wasn't sure what he would do if this wallet happened to be stuffed with cash. He had never found a wallet stuffed with cash before. There was only one way to find out.

Mister Bob opened the wallet. It opened along the spine like a book and it made him feel, despite everything wonderful that had happened, a sense of mild dissatisfaction that he had not yet turned a few pages that evening.

The wallet was not stuffed with cash.

The wallet contained a single twenty-pound-note with the queen's head on it. Scottish notes usually had the head of Robert the Bruce or Robert Burns or Nan Shepherd, not the British Queen. This wallet presumably belonged to an Englisher, which surprised Mister Bob since the train had not yet crossed the border. It belonged to someone making a return journey then, he supposed.

He flipped through the pockets in search of identification. A credit card revealed the name S SINGH, which was a fairly anonymous name really and not entirely helpful. An old family photograph crammed into one of the more miscellaneous wallet slots, however, was more helpful.

The photograph showed a young family, two parents and three children, standing in front of a large gorilla.

Mister Bob recognised the gorilla first.

It was a giant King Kong statue that used to stand in the Birmingham Bullring, back when Mister Bob himself was a child.

Mister Bob put the wallet in his mouth, clamped between his teeth epileptic-style, before remembering that it had been on the toilet floor, and was probably all uriney. He kept it clamped though, harm already done, while he unbuckled his belt and dropped his borrowed polyester railway company trousers.

The end of his penis was still a bit jizzed. The crab's eye gave a knowing wink.

Mister Bob, having shared something magical with his crustacean companion today, winked back.

Mister Bob sat on the toilet and the poo instantly fell out of his body. He felt it uncoil from his guts quite suddenly like the cord being tugged all the way out of a school gym bag.

This being a railway company toilet pan, there was no water in the toilet and no plop. The poo just fell with a dull thud onto an aluminium surface. Mister Bob wasn't entirely sure that the poo hadn't brushed against the back of his balls on its way down.

Mister Bob removed the wallet from his skull, making a satisfying *tack* sound as his teeth undug themselves from the leather, and he looked at the family in the picture again. His heart went out to them. Such love. Such true familial bliss.

The subject matter in the photograph had been trimmed from a larger photograph. Its shiny white back side had a repeating logo that read SPIELMANN⟩180.

The eldest child in the photograph was perhaps twelve years old, so this was a moment captured just before things would have become awkward and, if what Mister Bob knew about family life was universal, the family began to think differently to each other and to emotionally, inevitably and against free will, drift apart.

Mister Bob didn't recognise the adults in the photograph but he recognised the middle child, a small boy, aged perhaps ten or eleven, in a topknot. It was his horrible boss, Sunny.

Young Sunny was laughing. He was in love with life. He loved his parents and his sister and his brother and he loved the statue of King Kong.

Sunny was the boy in the topknot. The boy in the topknot was Sunny. Holy shit.

Mister Bob was so astonished by the spectacle of his boss as a smiling child that didn't notice the old woman in the background with the headscarf and the carrier bags. It was Scotch Gran doing the shopping.

Mister Bob sniffed. What, in the intervening years, had happened to turn the boy in the topknot into such a whingeing dickbag? It was one for the ages.

Mister Bob wiped his bum.

Mister Bob's day-long hangover was beginning to subside. He felt warmed, internally, by the wonderful events of the previous evening and by the curious time portal into '70s Birmingham where the Mighty Kong and the Singh family had stood in gleeful happiness.

Some seagulls noisily fought on the station concourse over an exploded packet of Really Cheesy Wotsits.

Mister Bob's salivary glands prepared his mouth for vomit as he watched one of the vulgarite birds gulp an orange cheese puff down, but, thankfully, he was not quite moved to retch.

As with any career alcoholic, Mister Bob knew that any hangover incurred during a drinking session, whether exacerbated by a stag party and an erotic encounter with a member of the railway company's cleansing team or otherwise, was temporary.

All manner of "hangover cure" had been concocted during the course of history, Mister Bob understood, and he was familiar with various ones from literature including Jeeves' eggs and worcestershire sauce and Hemmingway's absinthe-and-champaign afternoon punishment. In Mister Bob's opinion, nothing really cured a hangover. You just had to weather the storm.

Mister Bob's favourite way to weather the storm was with the assistance of Alka-Seltzer.

In the year 2019, however, and late in that year to boot, Alka-Seltzer was on its way out. Like baths, Alka-Seltzer was old-fashioned, indulgent, and too much fuss. Just as luxurious soaks in the tub had moved over to the businesslike rinses of power showers, Alka-Seltzer had been replaced in the mainstream consciousness by cold, efficient pills.

Mister Bob didn't want to take a pill, God damn it. Mister Bob wanted Alka-Seltzer.

He wanted to hear the comforting plink-plink as the two machine-pressed tablets hit the sides of the glass.

Unfortunately for Mister Bob, as well as this being 2019 in the year of someone's lord, it was also Central London and his stash of Alka-Seltzer tablets was sitting in a kitchen cabinet next to the jar of "prisoner" aspirin tablets, some nine-hundred miles up the East Coast Main Line.

Via Peterborough, Doncaster, York, Mister Bob thought reflexively and in an almost Pavel-like way, *Darlington, Durham and Newcastle.*

He didn't consciously think of those station stops. They just burst into his mind like home invaders. The repetitive world of work had wrecked Mister Bob and he wondered if the mechanism responsible for these uninvited place names was also responsible for the Panic Visions. He was having fewer and fewer of those now though. Since he'd started bathing, Mister Bob was far less troubled by Panic Visions, so he pushed their analysis out of his mind. Besides, he wanted to get some storm-weathering Alka-Seltzer.

There was nothing for it. He'd have to visit Babish. That's what Babish was for. He had packets of Alka-Seltzer in his stockroom that dated back to the moon landings.

After a pained trundle along the Euston concourse and through the early morning crowd of rat race ratters, Mister Bob arrived at the shop. The orange-coloured, somehow civic-minded 1970s lettering above the door, BABISH, made him feel immediately calm. The door-entry thing went BLOO-BLEEP! mechanically as he walked in.

"Morning Babish," said Mister Bob tiredly.

There was the usual pantomime ritual of Babish professing not to recognise Mister Bob but it seemed somehow less pronounced than usual. Maybe Babish had finally remembered him well enough to almost recognise him on the first attempt.

"Good morning, sir," said Babish, barely looking up from the documents he was signing with a tiny wooden pencil pilfered from IKEA, "what can I do you for?"

"Alka-Seltzer," managed Mister Bob, "and a bottle of mineral water."

"Oh," said Babish with a tone of recognition, "it's like that, is it?"

"Like what?" said Mister Bob pointlessly.

"Can't I interest you in a little hair of the dog?" said Babish and he produced a bottle of shit whisky from under the counter.

"No thank you," said Mister Bob, but secretly wishing beyond all reasonable depth to snatch the bottle from Babish's stock-soiled hands, "Just the mineral water and the Alka-Seltzer please."

While Babish was fetching the requested items, Mister Bob's mind returned briefly to the rat race types he'd pushed his way through in front of the railway station. His life was entirely at odds with theirs. He and they had practically nothing in common and occupied completely different worlds. The lives of people like Samuel Aitch Hargreeves were latitudinal while Mister Bob's was longitudinal. He worked through the night while they worked through the day. They travelled into London from within the commuter belt, usually from east or west, while he travelled between north and south all the way up and down the length of the Kingdom. They knew absolutely nothing of his life and he knew little of theirs. He expected many of them were hungover, so at least they shared that much. They also shared lives dominated by work, by a desperate coming and going. He doubted whether they drank through a whole day and a whole night very often though, and under such strange, unmoored circumstances.

Babish presented Mister Bob with a bottle of Evian and a friendly sky-blue packet of Alka-Seltzer. Together they looked like peace.

"Is that all for ya?" asked Babish.

Almost to be polite, Mister Bob ran his tired eyes over the junk covering Babish's shop shelves. He was about to say "yes" when his eyes locked on what looked like an old radio.

"How long has that been there?" asked Mister Bob on the assumption that the radios and other assorted junk had been there since the War.

"That?" said Babish, "It's new. Just came in. Hipster radio, innit."

Mister Bob didn't know what "hipster" meant but he supposed it was a youth culture like the "goths" he sometimes saw floating around on the steps of city railway stations, but the way Babish said the word made it sound slightly pejorative.

The radio was bright orange in colour and had the look of an old-fashioned transistor model, the kind that Mister Bob's parents might have listened to when they were teenagers in the 1950s. It had a handle sticking out of its side.

"It's a wind-up," said Mister Bob.

"I'll 'ave you know it's completely legitimate," said Babish who had clearly been looking forward to trotting that one out.

"Clockwork I mean," said Mister Bob redundantly.

A wind-up radio was exactly what Mister Bob needed for bathtime. He had been told since boyhood that electrical appliances and water do not mix. That image of the scorched, no, *scalded*, child-sized skeleton in the bathtub occurred to him. Maybe the radio could help him to avoid the stupid news intrusions on 6Music somehow too. The thing just radiated possibility. He could see it now, parked orangely on the toilet cistern in his Portobello bathroom, dewy with condensation from the hot bathwater steam.

"Do you remember Trevor Baylis?" asked Mister Bob.

"Who's that, guvnor?" said Babish.

"Inventor of the wind-up radio. He was on the television a lot when I was a boy," said Mister Bob, "Wind-up radios, well-well. Good idea. It was supposed to be for Third World countries really."

Mister Bob wondered if the United Kingdom would yet or would ever qualify as a Third World country. The wind-up radio being marketed here seemed to say it was so. As did those waterlogged lowlands and the sort of thing Katherine Cracknell liked to tell him about.

"I'll take it," said Mister Bob, and pulled the wind-up hipster radio from the shelf.

Mister Bob sat on the 17:34 to Waverley with the wind-up hipster radio neatly on his lap. The birds and animals and scarecrows blurred alongside him in the paddocks. He also saw the charred remains of a lightning tree and various small outbuildings for livestock to shelter in when it rained.

He had chosen a cramped and backwards-facing two-seat unit—seats B45 and B46—which was precisely the sort of seating arrangement most people would want to avoid. It was Mister Bob's preference though. The ill fit and the way that the seat-back tray pressed against his belly gave him a feeling of wedged-in security, plus he had found over the course of hundreds if not thousands of train journeys that he actually enjoyed the sensation of being pulled backwards along the rail for reasons he couldn't quite put his finger on. The way his right buttock spread onto the aisle seat from his ostensible position by the window probably meant that nobody would want to sit next to him, which was fine by Mister Bob. He wanted solitude above almost anything at this moment in time. It had been a strange few days. An unusually *sociable* few days. There was much to mull over.

Mister Bob had been flying high from the best thing that had ever happened to him: a long dreamed-of romantic entanglement on the *Magnificent Caledonian Sleeper*. It had been wonderful, wonderful. And he smiled warmly as he thought about it now. The cat's-tongue roughness of Tracey's feet. The way his muck had squirted merrily in her direction like the spritz of a fork-tined shellfish.

Yet only a few hours earlier, he'd been smacked rudely on the seat of his trousers by Sunny. At the time, it had felt almost like a reasonable thing to happen. After all, Sunny was a bastard and a twat. It was the sort of thing he would do. On the other hand it was an assault. An assault committed against a team member by a supervisor. It was bad news. It was one of the worst things that had ever happened to Mister Bob and the fact that he had accepted it as the sort of thing that happened to people like him only went to show how low Mister Bob had fallen in life, how little he thought of himself. He should probably take some sort of action. He should go to railway company HR. But would he be believed? And would there be any point? Mister Bob had no idea, but as he dwelled on it now, the warm feelings inspired by his moment of perfect romance moved over to feelings of anxiety and dread and doom, doom, doom.

The skies across the fields were burning orange,

which was strange because it was relatively early in the day. But things had been generally unseasonable of late —hadn't they?—and Mister Bob had long ago lost all sense of connection with how nature worked.

Mister Bob wondered if maybe women were better at understanding nature than men were. He was suspicious of any claim about women being innately better disposed towards something than men or vice-versa but this one seemed plausible to him. It must be something to do with their menstrual cycles, the way they synchronised with those of other women or were somehow related, tide-like, to the phases of the moon. Mister Bob had heard something along those lines and it hadn't seemed so dubious to him. Tracey, wherever she was right now, would probably be looking up at that orange sky, admiring it perhaps, and at peace with her innate understanding of it. That was if she wasn't hunched over the aluminium pan of a passenger toilet somewhere, under orders to scrub the cack out of it.

Only hours before his being assaulted by Sunny, Mister Bob had been drinking beer and vodka jellies in a remote northern city. It had started out well enough and according to plan but it had spiralled out of control when the lads had come along and taken a shine to him. These three events—the strange bender, the assault, the romantic entanglement—were all quite extreme and unusual in Mister Bob's otherwise prosaic life of books and trains and, most recently, bathtubs. They blurred together now in his memory and in his imagination and it made him feel sick.

Bathtub, bender, trains, buttwhack, footjob, book.

Mister Bob idly turned the handle of the wind-up hipster radio as it sat on his lap, already feeling like a dutiful little friend, and transferred some kinetic energy, transferred some of his calories and his *life*, into it.

Mere hours before the drinking spree, he'd been at home, in his flat, eating a hard-boiled egg in the kitchen and looking forward to the day ahead. This accounting of a two-day period made no sense: boiled egg, drinking bender, assault, romance, and now a return journey with a radio on his lap. What did it all mean? Life was nothing but chaos, random elements. His head span.

The wind-up hipster radio winked at Mister Bob.

Hole. Aperture.

It was for headphones, of course. And he'd already noticed that there was a pair of wired headphones curled up behind a plastic flap, which he'd originally thought was a battery cover. Mister Bob could listen to the radio right now, on the train, if he wanted to. He prised off the plastic cover, plucked the headphones out, untangled them clumsily but ultimately successfully and popped the headphone jack into the socket. The jack clicked in the socket with a satisfying sense of rightness.

Mister Bob plugged the earpieces into his ears where they rested slightly absurdly, almost too small for his mighty ear holes. They would have been manufactured for younger, less distended and bacon-like ears, he supposed.

But the sound was coming through.

"This is the 6Music News at six o'clock with me, Katherine Cracknell..."

Oh good, thought Mister Bob. *Hello Katherine Cracknell.*

"A state of emergency has been declared in the central belt of Scotland this evening as the International Space Station makes an unplanned re-entry into the Earth's atmosphere."

Bathtub, bender, trains, buttwhack, footjob, book.

Mister Bob's very essence lurched upwards in his body as if he were himself in free fall.

Once, when he'd been running home to mother's from Scotch Gran's, he'd misjudged the height of a wall and not realised his plight until he had fallen halfway down to earth. This, he realised with a sense of connectedness to past years, felt like that.

"Projections by NASA and the European Space Agency," said Katherine Cracknell, "concur that the most probable place of touchdown is the town of Lockerbie in the Scottish county of Dumfries and Galloway. Local police have confirmed that efforts are underway to evacuate the area."

This can't be happening.

Mister Bob's head span again.

He felt like he was tied up with wire, with electrical cable, with electrician's tape.

Spinning, spinning.

The sky! Of course, this is why the sky was so brightly orange. The sky was *burning*. It was on fire.

Who knew what fuels and chemicals had been in that thing, had been orbiting safely for twenty years and were now burning through the sky, burning on atmospheric re-entry?

"Canadian astronaut Captain Chris Hadfield," said Katherine Kracknell, "visiting London today as part of the Infinite Monkey Science Festival had this to say."

"It's the worst news I have heard in all of my life," said Captain Chris Hadfield. "An unspeakable tragedy. I was aboat to speak to the good people of the Leicester Square Theatre aboat my wonderful life aboard the station and now this. I'm gobsmacked, appalled. Would you like to hear my rendition of David Bowie's Starman?"

Mister Bob looked around the train carriage. A young woman with a nose pimple listened to music on her phone. An old lady in a knitted shawl read something on an Amazon Kindle. A man who looked like Sven-Göran Eriksson was reading an improbably large tombstone of a book by James Patterson. They all looked perfectly comfortable and content. Why wasn't anybody panicking?

"The Leader of the House of Commons at Westminster," said Katherine Kraknel into Mister Bob's bacon ears, "is on record as quipping with reference to Lockerbie that lightning really can strike the same place twice. There have been calls led by Ian Blackford of the Scottish National Party and Caroline Lucas of the Green Party of England and Wales for Mr. Rees-Mogg to resign. In other news..."

In other news?!

Mister Bob plucked the earbuds from his ears. He felt that, somehow, he would not be able to breathe if they stayed in.

Something almighty was happening, something *big* was coming down on all of us, something was glowing and tremendous and all-encompassing in its devastation, yet all that anybody in power could do was to quip and bicker and resign or refuse to resign.

Doom, doom, doom.

Somehow, it felt like everything had been building up to this. Leaping from that wall as a boy, having his boiler repaired, telling Mrs. Buntapples what was what, his great romance with Tracey, each exchange with Pavel in the hallway, his boiled egg, Sunny's clipboard, Brexit, Ebola. It was all, somehow, here. It was all happening *now*. He felt realer, more real somehow, than he ever had before. He felt like a person in the background who had become, for one shining and unasked-for moment, a protagonist.

Knock-knock-knockin' on Heaven's Door.

Mister Bob didn't know what to do. Should he cause a scene? Should he prise himself from seat B45, clamber across seat B46, and shout to the other passengers that the sky was, for real this time, falling down?

He couldn't. There was no point anyway. Nobody could help him. Nobody could help anyone.

Doom, doom, doom.

Mister Bob looked out of the window and across

the fields. They were remarkably empty fields; no livestock and no crops, just the occasional boundary marked by a drystone wall or a lonely tree. A ruin of a small castle or fortress squatted on the horizon, silhouetted against the blazing sky. Mister Bob had seen this roofless edifice many times before but had never remembered it for long enough to look it up in an encyclopaedia at home and, as such, had never learned what it was. It was probably too late now. The train wasn't near Lockerbie, the predicted site of renewed devastation, but he knew somehow that everyone was wrong, that the falling Thing wouldn't land where it was supposed to land, that the evacuation would be a waste of everyone's effort and panic, that there was only one place that the falling Thing was destined to land and that was squarely on Mister Bob's head. He knew it. He had always known it. He was knock-knock-knocking on Heaven's door.

Mister Bob's gaze shifted upwards from the site of the ruined castle or fortress and into the blazing orange clouds. He could see something.

Oh God, no.

It was unmistakable.

The solar panel was twisting and turning, dancing almost gracefully.

This was really happening. It didn't look like anything from a disaster movie, not that Mister Bob had seen many of those, but like something elegant in its evil, an avenging angel, Lucifer himself on wings of fire and light.

Falling, falling.

Closer to Earth.

Closer and closer to Earth.

Mister Bob recognised that his breathing had gone haywire. It felt like his chest was about to explode. Mister Bob closed his eyes and waited for it all to be over.

"We are now *fuzz-fersing* into Edin-*fuzz* Waverley," said the announcement, "ten minutes late. This was due to parts of the International Space Station having fallen on the line. We apologise for *sst-fuzz-ferst* this may have caused. *Kucka-chunk*."

It was a full two hours—long after Mister Bob had flashed his bus pass to the driver of the 124 and spent half an hour peering through the yellow-tinged windows in fear of seeing additional pieces of falling shrapnel, and still long after speed-walking past Mike's Fishing Tackle Shop with his polyester railway company uniform jacket pulled taut over his head as if railway company polyester might provide adequate protection from a burning hunk of artificial gravity generator—before Mister Bob understood fully, in his gut, that he'd had a panic attack. A panic attack triggered by a Panic Vision.

There was no world crisis. Not in reality. Katherine Cracknell had not spoken to him through the wind-up hipster radio. The International Space Station was as fine and intact and as orbitty as an International Space Station could possibly be. Mister Bob had not seen a burning piece of solar panel in the sky.

Parts of Mister Bob's (well, David McManaman's) polyester railway company uniform were strewn about in the hallway and on the bedroom floor of Mister Bob's (well, Mrs. Cuntapples') flat. Mister Bob was a man who owned neither the home in which he lived nor the clothes he wore. Did he own *anything*? Well, he owned a thousand dusty books. But could one ever be said to own a book? Given that someone else wrote it and that, after you die or simply tire of the book, it will be passed on to someone else, the best one could say about book ownership was that you were a temporary custodian. Mister Bob was happy enough to be a custodian of so many fine books, the vanilla-like smell of their billion pages now entering his nostrils and helping to restore him to a sense of basic anchoredness.

Mister Bob had tugged off the Clarks shoes (which he actually owned) and the sweat-soaked socks (which he also owned) and the crackling-with-static trousers as soon as he'd crossed the threshold of the flat and into the hall and then semi-slipped on the latest glossy announcements from the good people at Farmfoods. Potato smiley faces were half-price and there was twenty percent off minty peas.

Mister Bob's shirt was in the bedroom, thrown through the door in exasperation as soon as he'd been free to pull his arms from the sleeves. He'd tossed his necktie like a streamer across the bedroom and it now lay like a sleepy snake across the corner of the foot of his bed.

Mister Bob himself sat, scrunched up and naked, a pink ball, in the hallway, leaning against the slatted doors of the boiler cupboard. The sensation of the beige shag carpet beneath his bum was comforting; it reminded him of childhood moments spent hiding in the bottom of his wardrobe or auditing his shoebox of Britain's Knights on the similarly shaggy carpet in front of Scotch Gran's five-bar heater. This might only be a rented flat but it felt like home. Home is where you can sit, naked, on the floor and contemplate the sensations of carpet upon your sphincter.

Just before Mister Bob had hit the ground, he'd caught a glimpse of the dusty Yellow Pages and the even dustier blue Thompsons Local business directory in the bottom of the boiler cupboard. Why did he still have those? He had never really thought of himself as having them. They belonged to the flat. He could imagine Mrs. Cuntapples deducting money from his security deposit if he ever chucked them out (or indeed if he ever moved out and had the audacity to reclaim his deposit).

Breath finally steady, Mister Bob glanced over at the bedroom where his shirt lay, sweat rings around the armpits, and where he knew, but could not see from his low vantage point, the necktie to be strewn. The bed, Mister Bob was surprised to see, had been made. It was a rare thing that it should be made, but he remembered now, through the fug and buzz of Panic Vision, that he had made it before leaving for work and his drinking binge. The neatly-made bed was trigger enough for him to remember the calm he'd felt before it all kicked off. He would never have imagined that such a calm and leisurely morning could have been the prologue to a panic of proportions far greater than any he'd experienced before. A panic *attack*.

Yes, a panic attack. That's what it was. "Panic attacks" were something he'd heard people talk about. Panic attacks were real. Whatever was wrong with Mister Bob—whatever had long been wrong with him— was a normal thing. A horrible, life-sapping thing, but normal nonetheless. Normal things fit into the world. A person could treat normal things, or read about them, or read about people who suffered the same way while nodding in recognition. A person could even, theoretically, talk about these normal things with someone else, who might suffer the same way and nod in recognition. Normal things were visible to other people. And normal things could be treated. Normal things, Mister Bob reasoned, could be overcome if he could find it within himself to be clever and dedicated instead of self-destructive and pooped.

"Clever and dedicated" were not words many people would use to describe Mister Bob.

But those people didn't know that Mister Bob had a secret weapon at his command in the struggle to Get Better.

Mister Bob shifted his weight from his buttocks to his knees and the palms of his hands and he crawled like a grotesquely oversized baby towards the bathroom. He groped for the nearest bar of luxury soap, which happened to be SNOW FAIRY (GODDESS was now lost in Dundee along with his lieutenant Mister Matey) and he inhaled of it deeply.

Mister Bob felt his shoulders de-hunch.

The hack who had written that magazine article about—what was it called again?—self-care probably had a point about commercialisation, Mister Bob supposed, but he'd take it. The baths had really helped him. But helped him to do what? Get on track to a full-blown panic attack that had lasted somewhere in the region of three and a half hours?

Mister Bob did not know how long a panic attack could be expected to last but this struck him as excessive. Usually, his Panic Visions, as he called them, lasted only a few seconds. But he'd been inside this Panic Vision for hours and it had felt completely indistinguishable from reality. He was accustomed to the rising panic of an idea that *felt* real for a while and he was accustomed to the oddness of a fleeting vision, but a three-hour slip into an alternate dimension was something altogether different.

Mister Bob sighed. He closed his eyes and tried to sense what was around him by way of leaving his body and his crazy mind for a moment. Somewhere in the building he could hear a dog, Mrs. Cuntapples' little dog he supposed, yipping and yapping. He could hear light traffic outside. He could hear seagulls screeling in the Portobello sky. He could hear... the metallic clink of his letterbox opening. Mister Bob opened his eyes.

Nudely and pinkly, he peered around the bathroom door just in time to see the letterbox slapping shut. Odd.

January

Eight

Though he couldn't quite bring himself to consciously admit it, Mister Bob's life was slowly, by increments, improving.

And yet he wasn't happy yet. Not exactly. For starters, he had a sense that his Panic Vision—the Big One with the orange skies and falling shrapnel—was still within him. It felt like it was held behind a bulging door somewhere in his mind, the bolt and hinges holding but tentatively. The only solution he knew was to ignore it, day after day, and hope that it stayed behind that door and ate itself.

He still hadn't found the courage to find out how he looked without his stupid moustache and he still escaped into strange old books that nobody else bothered to read anymore, barely remembering any of the details once he'd finished them. He read these book at night, at home in his bed, and also by day when he was sitting on trains for ten hours at a stretch. In particular, Mister Bob's latest Stendahl was an unfinished novel called *Le Rose et le Vert* or *The Pink and the Green*. It was about a young heiress who is disgusted by money and has too many suitors. Mister Bob was unsure what to make of this one and he didn't understand what the title could mean, but he could relate to the central character's misgivings about money.

Mister Bob still wore his polyester railway company uniform (a replacement) for each of his long commutes and therefore most of his waking hours. He had, however, bought a new pair of shoes on an Oxford Street mission and these ones didn't make him look quite so stuffy or foolish. He had also fully got the hang of wearing his necktie at its full length so he no longer looked like a prematurely aged schoolboy.

The previous week, Mister Bob had acquired a rubber duck, the ultimate symbol of bathtime bliss. His other acquisitions, the Lush soaps and the essential oils and the Mister Matey bubble bath, had been nostalgic and transformational but ultimately functional. The rubber duck, meanwhile, was totemic, a sort of talisman to declare that "baths happen here." He had placed it, sentinel-like, on the moulded corner of the bathtub.

He was proud, too, of the way he'd acquired it. He'd gone to eBay for it because, every time he'd seen a rubber duck for sale in a shop, it had had the wrong look. Rubber ducks in the twenty-first century, it seemed, were too advanced. You could get ducks in scuba masks and ducks that looked like Wonder Woman or ducks wearing an Everton FC football strip, but you couldn't get ducks like the ones Mister Bob remembered from his childhood. As a boy, Mister Bob had a small family of bathtime rubber ducks: there was a big duck, a medium duck, and a little duckling. Three ducks, almost *Matryoshka*-like. They weren't rubber either, they were made of a relatively hard plastic and were hollow with small anus-like holes in the tail to squeeze out any bathwater. Just as computer-aided technology had deformed the face and shape of Mister Matey into a logic-free sailor boy, the same technology had made rubber ducks into quite complicated things. But he'd found the right one, with the right evocations, for just twenty quid on the Internet auction site. It had come to his Portobello door in a satisfyingly cube-shaped box. The duck had emerged from the packing peanuts, golden and friendly, untarnished by time or the presumably thousands of baths it had taken before it had reached Portobello.

It was the correct duck.

The best development of all, however, was that Mrs. Cuntaples had sent "a wee man" to repair his boiler once and for all.

To prepare for the wee man coming over, Mister Bob had cleared away all of the Farmfoods and Domino's Pizza junk mail from the floor of his hallway.

There was so much of it that, at first, it had been like shovelling snow. But by the time it was all in a single pile, it hadn't seemed like so very much at all. He tidied it all up into a neat stack in the way a TV news anchor might tidy up their important-but-probably-blank paperwork, and tossed it into the recycling bin under the kitchen sink. It took Mister Bob fewer than three minutes to achieve this and he briefly wondered why it had taken him so many *years* to get around to such a basic job.

While the wee man was repairing the boiler, he opened the boiler cabinet and taken note of the low pressure as advertised by the dial. He said something like "haven't you repressurised this?" to which Mister Bob remarked that it was not his job to maintain a boiler that wasn't his property and then he went off into his bedroom and closed the door. When he did this, Mister Bob was careful not to slam the door offensively. He didn't want to continue a conversation about boilers just to be polite but he didn't want to offend the wee man either. This was another recent change to his personality. He no longer sat and listened and said "yes, I see, uh-huh, ah, um, yes" while secretly thinking about other things. Mister Bob now left the conversations he didn't care for.

Mister Bob no longer said "ah" and he no longer said "um."

Mister Bob no longer stank of root vegetables or any other unwanted odour.

Since his space station panic attack, Mister Bob no

longer had troubling visions of plane crashes or of people coming up behind him with a garotte.

And he even had the correct duck.

These changes, Mister Bob supposed, were ultimately down to his baths and the particular thoughts and memories that came to him while he was in the bath, surrounded by bubbles and with the pleasant scents of soaps wafting through his expansively flared nostrils. Those baths had led to important feelings of hope and a decisive vow to Get Better.

It would be wise to say it quietly, but Mister Bob was Getting Better.

The water roared forth, piping hot, into a bathtub Mister Bob had cleaned to a shine.

Bath foam bubbled up, giving off its light chemical aroma. He'd replaced his lost-at-sea (or, okay, in-Dundee) Mister Matey with a *Mrs.* Matey from the same Superdrug and explained to Mrs. Matey that her man had fallen overboard and was missing, presumed dead. There was no point crying about it because bubbles were needed here nevertheless. Mister Bob enjoyed taking his clothes off in front of Mrs. Matey. Mrs. Matey looked perfectly happy about it too.

Mister Bob put his hand in the water and stirred it back and forth to ensure an even temperature. As he did so, he imagined himself as a chef. He was the Head Chef of a highly-respected restaurant frequented by

High Society. He was famous among gourmands the world over for his wonderful bisques. Piping hot and with just the right balance of Mrs. Matey bubble bath and essential oils.

Another new thing to Mister Bob was lotion. He'd been back to Lush, only not the one on Oxford Street recommended to him by Babish but one in Liverpool Street Station, which was remarkably convenient to him since his work took him there quite regularly. He bought a selection of lotions and he would work them into his skin, into his scalp, into his eyebrows, into his taint, into his teeth.

The water in the bathtub reached what Mister Bob now knew through familiarity was a sensible temperature and volume. Mister Bob turned off the taps, squinting at them in a slightly threatening way lest they complain with a rough squeak or continue to drip. When they did not complain or continue to drip, Mister Bob said "I should think *not*" and gave a little chuckle. Everything was set up to serve him and not the other way around. He no longer made compromises.

Mister Bob dried his hand and forearm on his new towel—another recent acquisition to replace the tattered old one, which now lived under the kitchen sink, belatedly demoted to the rank of "rag"—and left the room momentarily to return with his mobile phone.

He'd installed the BBC Sounds app so he could listen to the radio while in the bath. This had replaced the wind-up hipster radio as his main way of playing music in the bath. The wind-up was great but it reminded him of his panic attack and it would only play live music. The app could play live broadcasts too, only he could also listen to archived versions that would allow him to skip the hourly news bulletins that made him feel nervous. He'd come to believe that the *idea* of these news interruptions, of not being able to relax into the music in case Katherine Cracknell should suddenly kick the door in, was what had stimulated the panic attack.

He tapped the tiny "play" icon on the screen. It didn't do anything at first so he tapped it again and then again. Eventually, the sound kicked in and it was, unfortunately, the 6Music News.

"...and Mister Johnson," said Katherine Cracknell, "remarked that while he remained sympathetic to all those affected by the Windrush Scandal, he refused to commit to a rollback of the much-criticised hostile environment policies originated by his predecessor Theresa May during her tenure as Home Secretary."

This frustrated Mister Bob and he felt himself inching inadvertently towards a Panic Vision but managed to hold himself back from it with controlled breathing. It was only the tail end of the horrible 6Music news, which meant that a full hour of uninterrupted music was about to begin, which was ideal.

When the music returned, it was an example of what might be called World music, Mister Bob supposed, with harps and other gloriously tinkling sounds that struck him as very relaxing and perfect for a prolonged soak in the bath.

Mister Bob gently placed the phone face-down on top of the closed wooden lid of the toilet seat. It was just beyond arm's length, which, Mister Bob decided, was A Good Thing, since he would not be tempted to fiddle with the frustrating device while he was submerged in bubbles and hot water. If a news bulletin came on, he could reach across and stop it but it would need to be a determined effort. No idle phone fiddling! He wanted to let his mind drift in pleasant directions while submerged beneath the perfectly warmed water.

The time had come for the submergence ritual. Mister Bob was still marginally cautious when it came to actually getting into the bathtub. Part of his concern was that the addition of his body would cause the bathtub to overflow, though he now knew that this wouldn't happen when the surface of the water only came up to the level of the aperture of the emergency overflow pipe. Another concern had been the idea of slipping and somehow smashing his teeth out on the side of the tub. That would be just his luck.

Lately, however, such fears did not come so easily and, taking a firm grip of the chrome handles, Mister Bob got his first leg over the side of the bathtub and into the water. The now-familiar sensation of the water being slightly too hot hit his cold foot, but he knew by now that it was just an illusion caused by his foot being so cold and that, soon, his body would acclimatise to bathwater of a perfect temperature. He brought his second leg over the side of the tub and sat down, the familiar sensation of his buttocks spreading out over the bottom of the tub. Buttocks and bottom, bottom and buttocks.

Mister Bob lay back into the water, which now came up and over his shoulders, and he relaxed. He closed his eyes and listened. The music from BBC Sounds provided a smooth sonic background while, in the sonic foreground, Mister Bob could hear small amounts of water glubbing into the overflow pipe as the water peacefully lapped against its aperture.

He felt Mrs. Matey's bath foam crinkle up against his shoulders as usual and he felt the now-familiar *squoinkle* sensation but somehow did not hear the sound of it as his skin and subcutaneous fat rumbled against the sides of the tub.

The music on the radio was beautiful, even divine. It involved harps and various other exquisite sounds he could not identify. It was not remotely like anything he'd heard before and he liked it very much.

The music turned into an artificially fuzzy announcement about the radio station's own programming and then the gentle-voiced disc jockey came in. "That was Alice Coltrane with Ptah the el Daoud, I think it's pronounced," said the Northern English accent, "and that is our featured album of the month. Next on Freak Zone is a touch of Scott Walker with Sunn O..."

Mister Bob had never before heard the names of any of these musical performers and he didn't know what was going on but he remained open to it all. His baths had opened a conduit within him that had formerly been blocked. Besides, the phone was too far away to do anything about it. He had no desire to get out of the water.

Mister Bob knew very little about music. Now, however, in the tub, he had both the time and inclination.

The white eye of the rubber duck seemed to encourage him to go deeper.

Mister Bob closed his eyes again and allowed his mind to expand outwards in all directions.

Nine

Mister Bob was on the bus from Waverley to Portobello again. His shift for the day, rattling down the coast from Oban in the rain, was done. Oban, he had discovered, boasted a sculpture called "the man in the bath," which depicted, as you might imagine, a man. In a bath. It was off the coast of the town, surrounded by water and inaccessible by foot but you could see it from a pathway behind a fancy hotel. He'd admired the sculpture from this pathway and decided, illogically, that it was an artistic tribute to his own wellbeing.

Now, on the bus, he looked out the yellowish window at Mike's Fishing Tackle Shop, all boarded up. Never mind. He felt good today, even though winter was finally underway after an unusually warm start and he'd taken to wearing the North Face coat again over his polyester railway company uniform.

Mister Bob had come to dislike wearing a coat over his polyester railway company uniform because it made him too sweaty and it instilled an ambient feeling of imprisonment. Despite the changes he had made these past few weeks, he still had little sense of style and he couldn't be certain that his choice of overcoat was fashionable or even acceptable in the modern world. Truly, he had no idea.

He was nervous that his choice of coat might cause someone, just a member of the public, to take offence to him. "Oi, baldy!" they might say. Or was he being unjustly paranoid? Was it a symptom of the apocalypse in his head, which still waited and rumbled behind that closed door, its poisonous vapours leaking out from around the jam? Then again, people *did* take pointless offence to him sometimes, like the time he'd walked past some holidaying English girls sunbathing in bikinis on Portobello beach one summer and one of their boyfriends had booted a football at him and told him to fuck off, you old perv. He'd barely glanced. He'd just been exploring the rockpools with a little net, admiring the cockles.

As he was thinking about the cockles and how he used to like to admire them, something buzzed in Mister Bob's trouser pocket. He knew it was his mobile phone but it still surprised him because, really, nobody ever called Mister Bob or sent him any messages even though he was Getting Better. Up until now, he had mostly used his mobile phone as a way to listen to BBC 6Music in the bath and as torch when unlocking his door at night, since Mrs. Cuntapples had the lights in the close turn themselves off automatically at 9pm, when they might actually be needed. When it came down to it, practically nobody wanted to buzz Mister Bob's trouser pocket.

Maybe this buzz was a sign, a sign that he really was Getting Better. Maybe he was entering a new phase of his life in which people actually wanted to talk to him since he smelled good, liked listening to music, and wore shoes that suited him.

He fumbled the phone out of the pocket, briefly noticing the warmth it had absorbed from his own thigh.

It was a text message. From Tracey.

Mister Bob smiled.

"Hope u liked ur late birthday present ;)," the text message said, "Mite not c u again tho. New job. More when I no."

Mister Bob felt as if someone had reached up into his body with pincers and pulled the living soul from the bottom of his trouser leg.

He felt like throwing up.

The text message was Tracey's way of saying there would be no more romance between them. It was her way of telling him that that was that.

Mister Bob was a balding, moustachioed bachelor.

Tracey was a bawdy queen.

Tracey would never experience the benefits of his new bathing regimen, how seriously he had taken her suggestion ("you know," she'd said, "rub-a-dub-dub"), and the effect she'd had on his life. She's missed out on his cleanliness and his golden shimmering last time thanks to the Dundee Incident and he hadn't seen her since. Sometimes their timetables just didn't line up for ages (though a month was an unusually long time not to see her and he fully expected that Sunny had had a hand in it).

Urgh. He'd been so stupid to have thought that anything that had happened between them was serious. She had been nice to him was all. She had taken pity on him. She had done a nice thing for a balding, moustachioed bachelor's birthday, which even he himself had forgotten.

Somewhere in his mind, a rusty old bolt slid. Wooden planks bulged and trembled. A hinge pinged off.

The sky above the bus, above Portobello, began to burn orange.

Mister Bob thought about Sunny, about the sensation of the clipboard hitting Mister Bob's buttocks. He remembered reeling with shocked disbelief but it was paradoxically coupled with a sense of normality.

He thought of his paunch, how he'd tried to capture the attitude of those healthy-minded body positivity women of the Internet. He'd accepted that he'd been living a life of being pushed around by wild forces beyond his control, but if it was *all* beyond his control he'd never be able to Get Better. All of this self-care, all of this bathing and the likes, had been a seductive idea but ultimately a waste of time and hope. It might work for other people but how could it ever work for Mister Bob? He'd been ridiculous to think it. The hack writer of that magazine has been right. It was just another way to sell junk to twats. Fancy soap in this case. And Mister Bob in this case.

Falling.

Falling.

f

a

l

l

i

n

g

.

.

.

At home, Mister Bob went to the toilet. As he pissed, he imagined the meat of his penis plopping out suddenly into the pan and lying there like a bright red sausage and colouring the water red.

The tube of skin still attached to his body rasped violently like an angry windsock.

He shrugged the Panic Vision off with a near-automatic calm. He had no time for Panic Visions inside other Panic Visions. Mister Bob drew a bath.

★

Mister Bob shed his clothes. He unbuttoned everything and it all fell to the bedroom floor in one big flop. *Faddup*, said his clothes as they fell to the floorboards.

The flat was nice and warm, the radiators pumping out their expensive heat, though Mister Bob's skin barely sensed the temperature of the air.

He'd once read that the people who live in Hawaii enjoy such a consistently warm and humid atmosphere that they were barely aware of where their skin stopped and the fresh Hawaiin air began and that this gave them, among all other human beings, a unique bond with the environment in which they lived.

Mister Bob had never felt any kind of bond with any environment in which he had lived. Mister Bob was more of an endurer.

But wasn't enduring a kind of strength too? A sort of admirable stoicism? Somehow the thought rallied him. Parts of his mind came back together, were reconstructed, like pieces of a jigsaw puzzle. He'd take control.

He'd take control.

He rolled, proverbially, his sleeves up. There was work to do.

Mister Bob would enjoy one last bathtime. And it would be a bathtime to remember. For at least ten minutes anyway, or however long the chemical process happened to take. He'd read that it could take about twenty minutes but it struck him intuitively as an unrealistically long time. Ten minutes was closer to what he expected.

He turned the taps and remembered how they used to complain with the effort of the twist before he had taken to Getting Better and getting clean and trying to become a healthy member of society that people would be happy to get into a lift with and might even want to talk to.

As the bathtub filled and the steam began to permeate the atmosphere of the bathroom, Mister Bob went off to the kitchen to release the prisoners from their jar. He peeled back the foil, rolling it back almost like the cover of a tin of sardines, and studied the pristine white number within. There were a good three or four fistfuls of aspirin tablets in the jar.

"Today, ah," said Mister Bob, "you are, um, free."

He smiled almost affectionately and shook the jar to hear their rattly sound. Memories of Scotch Gran and her little pebbledash council house and her unlikely garden leaping with frogs flittered briefly across his mind, giving him an involuntary smile. He placed the jar on the counter for a while and picked up the wind-up hipster radio to crank it up. He couldn't be bothered jabbing at his stupid phone screen again. BBC Radio 6Music kicked into gear. Some kind of maudlin Country-and-Westernish song about leaving your heart at the stile of a field. Whatever were the young people listening to now?

"Perfect," said Mister Bob, because, actually, it was just right. It suited the mood.

With the wind-up hipster radio in his hand and the prison jar tucked coolly beneath his clammy armpit, Mister Bob inched towards the bathroom.

Before he passed the threshold of the increasingly steamy room and submerged himself into the now-familiar but not so long ago alien sound of a filling bathtub, he looked around the rented flat from his position in the hallway. One last look.

Mister Bob looked first at some new pieces of unstoppable junk mail and his attention alighted briefly on some excellent crinkle-cut chip deals from Farmfoods.

He looked next at the boiler cupboard with its latticed door and remembered the trouble the boiler had given him during his initial forays into bathtime bliss. He admired the grey-tinged sunlight beaming through the living room's luxurious bay window and the way it scattered across the book-filled room. Dust had become caught in some of the sunbeams and he noticed that in addition to some loose flecks of dust there were one or two dust bunnies drifting in the air too. He wondered if dust bunnies often lifted off the floor or if today's particular January sunniness amounted to a Big Event, the dust bunny equivalent of a rocket launch. He glanced also into his bedroom, at the unmade bed, his erstwhile sty, and the impressive number of books that were stacked in piles upon the wooden floorboards and graced the canopy-like shelf above his headboard. He remembered an estate agent describing how to sell a house on the wall-mounted

TV screen of a pub somewhere, saying that small collections of books or objects were "cute" but that too many would suggest mental derangement and then you'd never be able to sell your house.

The world's books, he mused, even just the thousand or so here in the flat, contained so much wisdom and, more importantly, so many perspectives. Books were codified experience and a culminated legacy of a long-lived commitment to Renaissance Humanism. But what sense did that make in the context of the world now? Things were heating up. People were becoming more and more...

Mister Bob liked the people he read about in books but he could never find people like that in real life. Why? Why was that? Maybe the problem was inside him. Or maybe the world of work and managers and rush-rush-rush was just dragging everyone down and making everyone disgusted with everyone else and the authors of books hadn't caught up with that reality yet. Or maybe the books he was reading were too old so that the people he saw in them, like the light from stars, were so old that, in fact, they really didn't exist anymore. Maybe all the good people, the people who humoured other people, the people who spoke generously and made logical sense and made reasonable decisions, were all gone and that was that.

He put the difficult thoughts out of his head.

He was leaving the world just as it was meant to be.

And he was taking control.

Nothing is wrong here, thought Mister Bob, trying not to think about orange fiery skies or falling solar panels, *all is well and good. Everything is, by definition, as it should be.*

Fatalism had never been Mister Bob's favourite school of thought but he found himself reduced to it now, on the threshold of his bathroom, and in it he found a certain comfort.

Mister Bob went into the bathroom. He placed the wind-up hipster radio and the jar of prisoners-pending-release on the toilet cistern. He tenderly moved the yellow rubber duck from his sentinel position on the corner of the bathtub and into the water, placing the prison jar upon the spot vacated by the duck.

He tested the water, first with his elbow and then with his chilly foot, which struck him for the first time as being somehow made of pig. Mister Bob's foot didn't look like the foot of a pig—no trotter had he—but it looked somehow like it was made of swine matter. Not "pork" exactly, cooked or otherwise. Just pig material. He felt repelled by himself. He wasn't sure how or when he had become pig material.

The temperature of the water was optimal! A pleasant surprise. His thoughts of the world being just right today and of his foot being made of pig matter were blown out of his mind as if on a puff of wind. State memory certainly was something. The thoughts of past bathtimes did not yet come rushing back but they certainly teased and beckoned him.

It was confirmed in Mister Bob's mind that this was the correct state in which to leave; floating on an ocean of bathtub memories, connected at once with these temporal oases in his own past. He was also glad to have had the boiler fixed. He had at his disposal for this important moment the perfect water-heating machine.

Mister Bob unscrewed Mrs. Matey's hat and poured a generous helping of her internal resource into the bathtub. He also threw in a few scented oil sachets. He wanted this all to be perfect. He may have made a mess of certain things in his time on Earth, perhaps not risen to certain challenges in the way he should have done, but his exit was going to be just right.

The water in the bathtub was foaming gaily.

Mister Bob went back out to the hallway and unlocked the door. He didn't want them to smash the door down when someone worked out what had happened.

He wondered how those events would unfold. How would they find out? He was surprised not to have thought of this before. Would Mrs. Cuntapples come looking for his rent cheque? That was his favourite option. She deserved to find his beautiful bloated body. But as a landlady, she'd probably seen her fair share of lifeless floaters and wouldn't be too troubled by it. Which was fine by Mister Bob because he meant the rancid old bint no particular lasting harm. No, it was more likely that Pavel would smell a certain kind of smell and come to investigate. Or maybe someone, Sunny most likely, would notice that he hadn't reported to work and call the police station in Portobello or in some other way sound the alarm.

However it would happen, he didn't want to cause any inconvenience to anyone or to damage Mrs. Cuntapples' door. So he unlocked it, shivering with a slight sense of vulnerability.

He retreated into the bathroom. The maudlin music had moved on to something less maudlin but similarly Country. Something about an old jug being last seen down near a well. It confused him a little but it was fine. He didn't want to get into radio tuning now. Enough foaming water in the tub, Mister Bob closed the taps. Everything was set.

Control, control, he was taking control.

He had not brought a glass of water with which to swallow the aspirin tablets. He knew he would need more than a single glass. His plan was to drink the bathwater. It made perfect sense to Mister Bob. He would become one with his bathwater, inside and out, bubble-bath and scented oils and all.

Something clanged and rumbled outside. A docking clamp perhaps. Another solar panel. One of those suction toilets he supposed they must use, just like the ones on trains. Mister Bob couldn't control any of *that*. But he could control what was happening *here*.

He tested the temperature of the bathwater one last time. Forgetfully and slightly anxiously he used his hand for this. Absently, he turned and dried his hand on the towel, which hung on the bathroom door. Returning to face the bathtub again and touching the rim of the prisoner jar with one finger, Mister Bob....

crack

The world erupted and then blanked out for a second like an interrupted radio signal.

The back of Mister Bob's head was suddenly in pain. His coccyx hurt too and he didn't know what he was looking at for a while until he realised it was a shape in the soft artex of the bathroom ceiling. Sideways, it was plausibly raccunk-shaped and he thought for a moment that his old friend had come back to see him. But why was he looking at the bathroom ceiling at all? He was supposed to be killing himself with a lethal combination of lovingly hoarded aspirin tablets and slightly toxic but perfectly-heated bathwater.

Mister Bob had slipped on the bathmat.

He sat up a little and touched the back of his head. There was blood on his hand. He must have hit his head against the side of the bathtub or perhaps on the metal door handle as he'd come down.

Blood. On his hand.

What?

Mister Bob passed out.

Mister Bob came to. He wasn't sure how long he'd been unconscious. Perhaps it had been an hour. But the song about the old jug and the well was still playing so either this was a runaway hit that the radio station played by the hour or he'd only been out for a few seconds. There were prisoners everywhere.

He could feel things closing in on his vision again when a voice spoke to him.

"This... is... K a t h e r i n e... C r a c k n e l l,"

it said, all stretched out and distorted, "And this is the 6Music News."

No, thought Mister Bob, *not now for crying out loud.*

"Two members of the same British family have tested positive for the coronavirus, the chief medical officer for England has announced," said the newsreader, "The novel coronavirus, which was first reported on New Year's Eve in Wuhan, China..."

What? thought Mister Bob, *the novel...*

Mister Bob died.

How I Wrote *Rub-A-Dub-Dub*: An Indulgent Afterword

Look, I'm not sorry about the ending. I like it when novels end abruptly, almost as if they've run out of tape, and there aren't very many that do. It's good that we'll never know if Mister Bob went through with his suicide attempt.

The way Mister Bob goes out is consistent with his concerns about free will, of not being in control of his own destiny. It was tempting to temper the effect by adding a coda about Mister Bob in the afterlife, meeting the Giant Rubber Duckie in the Sky or something, but I didn't want to blunt the finality of his exit-by-bathmat. Fatalism might not be Mister Bob's favourite school of thought but the nature of his exit was inevitable. There was also the temptation to make it clear that the ending wasn't real at all but a Panic Vision. Maybe it *was* a Panic Vision. I'll never tell.

The abrupt ending is one of my obsessions. Some of my other obsessions are also in the novel: the not-entirely-consensual nature of work, workplace indignities, and finding what I call comedy in what others might call "nothing."

It started in the bath. Well, obviously. I noticed how the thoughts would come and go against a canvas of very little. They were less associative and fractal than my usual everyday thoughts and, instead of zipping all over the place in their usual caffeinated way, they had a tendency to bore down, go deep. I found myself thinking of childhood, usually with childhood bathtime as a starting point. I remembered the bath toys I had and then the moments around bathtime—Sunday evening rituals like my dad watching *Songs of Praise* on the television and us all screaming the house down when Harry Secombe came on with his horrible singing, my sister drying her hair at the fireplace—and then out into the street and into the world.

I found it difficult to remember the thoughts I'd had in the bathtub once I was out of it and drying off, but some of them would return to me when I next took a bath. The mischief of "state memory" was at work. Nevertheless, a thought I managed to capture was: *a whole book about bathtime.* It would be a challenge to write deep instead of wide, almost like

French phenomenological writing. There would be nowhere to hide, nowhere to scuttle off to when a scenario ran its course. Well, almost nowhere. You could descend into the past, into rumination, into self-analysis. The cheats were practically endless.

Most of the books I read for leisure are novels and I'd long wanted to write my own. I felt as if I'd been building up for a decade to writing a novel, everything up to now being either practice or pragmatism. "What could I write *now*?" has always been my starting point and the answer, until now, had never been "a novel." At last, I felt ready. I'd find a way to convert bathtub journalism into a novel. But could I write a whole novel set in a bathtub? Yes, but I'd have to cheat a lot.

One of the cheats was to create a world for all this to take place in, a place to go that wasn't the bathtub. For contrast, it would be a grimey world of dirt and sweat and turpitude. I didn't want his job to be in a boring office so I put him on the trains. The sleeper service Mister Bob sometimes works is an exaggeration of the long-distance commutes many of us have faced as wage slaves. I wanted his circumstances to be extreme, to verge on magical realism, like when John Cusack gets his filing job on "the eleven-and-a-halfth" floor of an office building in *Being John Malkovich*.

If this was to be a pure storytelling enterprise, I wanted to create a new character. A way to do that, I decided, was to shift my perspective. I didn't feel ready to venture into non-male or non-white experience, getting a hundred things embarrassingly or offensively wrong, so I came up with something else: I'd be older. It didn't feel like such a leap. It was more predictive than fictive. Besides, an older and balder and fatter man (a figure I'm slowly turning into anyway) would look good in the bath. Oliver Hardy, all soapy and half-submerged is a lovely image. Stan Laurel? Meh. So that was the first thought that led to Mister Bob.

"Hoy! Mister Bob!" were the first words to stutter out, meaning the first person to speak in the novel wasn't my leading man but his neighbour, Pavel. But with those first utterances came our hero's name. I liked that it was a derivative of my own name. I also liked that this atypical variation on it, "Mister Bob" as opposed to merely "Bob," was the way he'd been introduced to us and, therefore, was the way he'd remain throughout the novel. The character's response to this mangling of his name and to his neighbour's over-familiarity could only be exasperation. Exasperation or defeatedness already suited him. It felt right and I ran with it. A character was born.

A way I wanted to illustrate the long-distanceness of his job, Mister Bob's passage from North to South and Back Again, was to use lots of regional accents. As the accents of passengers and colleagues changed around him, it would be obvious that we were moving from place to place. Plus, accents written down as "eye dialect" are funny and this was supposed to be a loosely comic novel. I ended up toning this down but many accents are still there.

I had a "Scotch Gran" in real life. She was my mother's grandmother from Kirkcaldy. She lived in a pebbledash council house in England with a garden through which frogs would hop on their way to a nearby brook.

Someone like Mister Bob also crossed my path in real life once. I didn't remember him until long after starting the book. It was in 2007. I know because I keep a diary and you can read about the original Mister Bob encounter at wringham.co.uk/the-tail

I once overheard a terrible conversation between two Virgin Rail employees about whether a child in a photograph was Chinese or had Down's Syndrome. That was real, I'm afraid. (I hesitated over its inclusion, but it happened and it's what some people are like: an aim of my novel was to represent a period of time between Brexit and the Pandemic and that really was the sort of bollocks you'd hear sometimes).

Mister Bob needed a horrible boss so I invented Sunny. I decided he should be from the Midlands by way of filling in some geography between the two main settings of London and Edinburgh, that he should be easily riled, thin-skinned. Sunny is working-class just like Mister Bob but more ambitious and a company man. Working life is full of such characters, those who want to get ahead either because they've been duped into a belief in meritocracy or because they can't see a way around their problems other than to climb the pole. Sunny is only inadvertently an antagonist; he's as much a victim of capitalism as Tracey and Mister Bob. I was born in Dudley and Sunny represents a certain attitude among the hard-working Midlanders I grew up with who thought that, despite everything, they might actually have been winning.

Each character in the book, with the possible exception of Pavel, is losing in their own particular way. I think I owe this to the novels of Patrick Hamilton. Moreover, humorist Jonathan Ames writes, "winning is good for fantasies and late-night insomnia, but losing is good for writing—it's more interesting, more humorous, more human" and I agree.

—RW, Partick, 2023.

Acknowledgements

For moral and material support I'm grateful to Eva Alisic, Josie Backhouse, Tommy Barr, Paula Billups, Tom Birch, Landis Blair, Tim Blanchard, Meadhbh Boyd, Arnold Brown, Sarah Burgess, Reggie Chamberlain-King, Apala Chowdhury, Suzanne Crimin, Angelene Darbyshire, Terri-Jane Dow, Caitlin Doughty, Jim Elliott, Scott Elliott-Brand, Gabriel Featherstone, Alex Frolov, Cristina Garriga, Henry Gibbs, Catrìona Goodrick, Martin Greaney, Jonny Hanna, Jan Haspeslagh, Louise Henderson, Chris Hendrie, Leonora Hennessy, Keir Hind, Roy Ibbotson, Holly, Graham, Marcus, Jackie Inch, Benn Kovco, Alex Leibner, Louise and Mark Leibner, Kirsten Levene, Tyron Love, Alexander Jorgensen, Patrick Germanier, Emily Gref, Jessica Gonzales, Robert Post, Fraser Smith, Rowan and Mark Smith, Ian Macbeth, Jamie Mactulloch, Johnston, Todd McKerchar, Louise McVey, Chris Miller, Marketa Muzikova, Katy Nicholson, Kat Rolley, Phil Scanlan, Stacy Shuda, Andrew Sinclair, Mason Singleton, Josh Skillman, Catherine Slater, Adam Snyder, Mark Stanley, Andrew Tapp, Steffi Tuemmers, Kirsty Turkington, McKinley Valentine, Karen Vaughan, Peter Vibert, Spencer Wakeling, Mark Wentworth, Sven Werner, and Bill Whitmer.

Special thanks to Mum and Dad, Samara Leibner, Mac MacGregor, and Ryan Vance.

Read more books at
www.poniesandhorsesbooks.com

Learn more about this author at
www.wringham.co.uk